THE
ABYSS OF
POSSIBILITY

Gordon R Clarke

SilverWood

Published in 2024 by SilverWood Books

SilverWood Books Ltd
14 Small Street, Bristol, BS1 1DE, United Kingdom
www.silverwoodbooks.co.uk

Text and images copyright © Gordon R Clarke 2024

ISBN 978-1-80042-258-2 (paperback)
Also available as an ebook

British Library Cataloguing in Publication Data
A CIP catalogue record for this book is
available from the British Library

Page design and typesetting by SilverWood Books

GORDON R CLARKE is an international authority on digital banking and financial policy. However, he also enjoys writing stories and poems, playing the guitar and performing in comedy revues. He has an MA in Natural Sciences from Cambridge University and a PhD in Applied Physics from City University in London. Born and brought up in south-east London, Gordon has worked in five continents for major consulting firms and his own Singapore-based company, and lived in eight countries, which creates the backdrop for his writing. He now spends his free time mainly in Thailand and Greece. During his career, he has published three technical books, many articles on behavioural economics, payment technology, cryptocurrencies and artificial intelligence and philosophical papers on science and religion. When a research student, he won a London Colleges short story competition, judged by the late Philip Larkin.

Having published his first book of short stories *Someone Else's Gods* in 2022, Gordon is pleased to present *The Abyss of Possibility* – his new collection – and plans to publish more fiction, while making the most of his wide range of interests from financial markets and science to music and creative writing.

To follow Gordon's blogs and discover more of his work, please see www.manandcyberman.com.

Also by Gordon R Clarke

Someone Else's Gods

Praise for Someone Else's Gods

"Gordon Clarke leads us through a series of stories and vignettes that are beautifully crafted, compelling to read, and infused with a sense of the unknowable beyond the surface of things. In the end it is the fullness of life itself that triumphs."

Lord Chris Smith, Master of Pembroke College, Cambridge

"This is such a good collection of short stories. Clarke starts conventionally enough with a twist in the tale story (only there are two twists), but then we find ourselves on terrific journey through (for example) exotic places, ten dimensional pizzas, artificial intelligence, the Christmas letter to end all Christmas letters, and a critique of contemporary society through an anthropological account of another, fictional (or is it?) society. In turn laugh-out-loud funny, disquieting, poignant and enlightening, Clarke's stories are cleverly crafted and have left this reader wanting more... so it's lucky that the book concludes with brief clips from another collection described as 'forthcoming'. Highly recommended."

Richard Ellis – British Central Banking expert

"Highly enjoyable collection of "bite sized" short stories. Gordon entertains us with his imaginative stories that range from summoning O'Henry to Arthur C. Clarke to the deeply personal and recollections of a dark time in recent history. Familiar situations often make the reader contemplative but there is much humour here as well. Recommended.

Matthew Rask – American Sound Engineer

To my children, Phaedra and Maritsa, who have inspired me throughout their lives and are now making their own way in the world creating their own stories

Contents

Preface

My stories explore the distinction between what is true and what seems to be true – a struggle we all face every day. Life can be a bit like a bad movie sometimes, with each small decision facing us with possibilities that seem like an abyss into which we could fall because of too little or too much information that may turn out to be fantasy, not reality. So film-making is a fascinating illustration of this theme, for what do movies do but challenge very directly the boundary between reality and fantasy?

The early film-makers, especially in the silent movie era, wove dreams to help ordinary people find a way to escape the everyday; to be carried away out of their humdrum lives. So directors like Cecil B. DeMille used hitherto unimaginable glamour, religious fervour, implied sex, and enormous movie sets to create imaginary worlds. It is no surprise that the outraged conservative forces who brought about Prohibition also tried to undermine the film industry by rumour and innuendo, sometimes aided by the press.[1] No small pleasures could be permitted to the masses, lest chaos ensue.

There are immediate comparisons today with the vast trove of disinformation that spreads on the internet (such as anti-vaccination conspiracy theories), encouraged by targeting algorithms spreading false witness, faked information and

---

1   I recommend the series *Paul Merton's Birth of Hollywood*. Note especially the persecution of Roscoe 'Fatty' Arbuckle, the popular colleague of Charlie Chaplin.

doctored photos. But ultimately, those silent stars were stabbed in the back by studio bosses more concerned with profit than with truth – the super-rich ruled the roost even then. Now it is worse. We have news media and social media run by billionaires who have unimaginable power over our information input and so drive the public perception of truth. One error of judgement by a social media mogul and we can be derailed from the track of truth in an instant. Promulgating lies and disinformation masquerading as 'free speech' is presented as a right; but is it not a pre-eminent human right to know the truth? To know what is really happening rather than what an algorithm wants us to believe?

So to my mind, our world is a far less comfortable place in which to live than it was a mere two years ago. First, the pandemic sliced through our pleasant existence, trailing divisive misinformation in its wake, and then, only a few days after the publication of my first short story collection, *Someone Else's Gods*,[2] a futile war based on historical fantasies broke out in Europe. No longer was the world an enlightened place, and the post-war 'Long Peace' had suddenly been smashed to pieces around us.

All the more necessary, therefore, to explore alternative realities through fictional characters and situations and stimulate an appreciation of what truth is – because truth is important. So in this new collection I hope you will enjoy meeting again some of the reality-juggling characters with whom we made an acquaintance last time, as well as some new companions to share our pilgrimage through the landscape of fact and fiction. *The Abyss of Possibility* contains some comedy which I hope will make you laugh out loud and cheer you up; some sci-fi with the message

2   https://www.silverwoodbooks.co.uk/someone-elses-gods-by-gordon-clarke

that, across the sum of all possible worlds, things could actually be worse – with or without artificial intelligence; and some pieces that address the conspiratorial fantasies that social media has spread into the mainstream.

But there are bright spots that have kept me going through these dark times. Reading Richard Holmes's wonderful biographies of the early nineteenth-century Romantic poets is one of them. That was an age in which we can all be delighted not to have lived – no Long Peace in those times. Holmes describes[3] a pair of Romantic European expatriates he met in Rome for whom 'the borders between remote possibility and the immediate practicalities of life had become permanently blurred'; an experience with which we can all have some sympathy today. Holmes goes on to explain that those gentlemen lived in a cognitive world consisting of what 'might have happened to them, what they wanted to happen rather than what actually happened'.

That kind of joyful escapism into the subjunctive is perhaps one solution that we can choose in a world in which lobbing high explosives into someone's living room, or murdering children with automatic weapons, has become an acceptable response to the pain of existence rather than the plainly criminal act that it is.

So we live in a world of war, but not of heroes. A world of intellectually barren leaders and massive cowardice. A world in which truth is sacrificed for profit, and sanity for atrocity. As a species, we need to think again. How do we prevent greed and injustice taking over national institutions and throwing us into the abyss of possibility? And so I present these tales to you in the hope that they will not only be a rollicking good read, but will stimulate the grey matter enough to mount more than a silent

---

3   In *Footsteps: Adventures of a Romantic Biographer*, by Richard Holmes, Harper Perennial, 2005, p168.

protest against greed and violence. A protest that is best expressed – as for Holmes's two Romantics – as what we 'wanted to happen rather than what actually happened'.

If we focus enough on what we want to happen, then maybe one day it will.

GRC
Cha Am, Thailand
November 2023

A Face in the Dark

AUGUST IN NORTH ISLAND New Zealand may not have been the best time for a visit to family. The night was chilly, and the two children were settled under the blankets in their twin beds in a plain but comfortable spare room. A single bedside lamp burned on the table between the beds, and shadows played across the ceiling. Their mother had said goodnight and gone downstairs to help her cousin make dinner. The man sat on the foot of the bed on the left, his face lightly illuminated by the lamp, like a Halloween lantern.

"Tell us a story, Daddy. Please, please tell us a story."

The man smiled, stood up and walked a couple of steps over to a high bookshelf stacked with children's books. "OK, which story would you like tonight?"

"No, not those, Daddy. Tell us one of your stories: the Yeti story," chorused the two children, girls of eight and six, always eager to listen to accounts of adventures that no one outside the family was going to hear. "Please tell us the Yeti story again."

He strolled back to the bed and sat down. This was a story that didn't need to be read from a book. "Right then. Settle down."

The children snuggled down, impatient. The soft light flickered eerily as the wind blew through the frame of the window and kissed the fringe on the lampshade. The man began to relate the tale, adjusted just a little for the age of his audience. He turned up the collar of his polo shirt against the draught and began.

"There was a group of climbers – six of them – who had set out to climb a peak in the Himalayas."

"Where's the 'alayas, Daddy?" asked Ellen, the older girl, her bright eyes shining in the lamplight.

"*Him*alayas. In the north of Nepal, on the Tibetan border with China. That's near India. Remember, I showed you on the map?"

"Ooh, yes. A long way away," said Mary, the younger girl. "I like maps."

"You could only reach the peak from the Nepalese side, because the paths were steep but passable and there was a base

16

camp area to set up tents and materials ready for the higher climb. Once the men reached the foothills of the western mountains, they entrusted their tough Japanese jeeps to the care of the elders of a quiet farming village. From there they carried most of their equipment in big backpacks." He paused for a moment to point at a backpack leaning against the wall behind him and made a broad gesture to indicate that the men's packs were very big. "They hired a couple of horses to carry the heavier items. Nepal was green and beautiful, full of cultivated fields, bubbling streams of cold, clear water, and tiny villages. At the head of many of the valleys was a temple. Some had a huge Buddha statue overlooking the valley from a hillside." He gestured again to indicate the size of the statues. "The only roads were narrow tracks across the jagged hills where few Western people ever set foot."

"Were there tigers, Daddy? Tigers? And bears?" asked Mary, who always wanted to know about the animals in his stories.

"Tigers are very secretive, so they didn't see any. But maybe there was something else…watching." He rocked his head from side to side, eyes wide.

"Ooh, go on, Daddy, go on!"

"So three nights later, after a slow ascent from the valleys through the most beautiful scenery, the climbers reached a small mountain village and decided to stop for the night. They sat round a fire in the village square with a group of local people to find out more about the mountain and to seek advice before the toughest part of their climb began.

"'You'll need porters,' said the boss of the village, who spoke English well because he had gone to a British school in Kathmandu. 'Our people will be pleased to help you, but of course you'll have to pay them handsomely, because there are risks in going into those mountains.'

"'We understand,' said the leader of the climbers. 'But the horses can't go much higher, and with six of us, we'll probably need three or four animals to transport our equipment.'"

The man leaned towards the children as he uttered the word 'animals' and widened his eyes.

"What kind of animals, Daddy?" The girls knew what was coming, but loved the sound of the words. They gazed intently at him, now sitting up in their beds despite the chilly air, rapt with attention as the story unfolded.

"Wait and see," whispered the man.

"Go on, Daddy," insisted Ellen, hugging her teddy bear for warmth.

"'Our people will help you, and we can look after your horses until you come back,' said the village boss with a sincere smile, indicating the stables across the square. 'In recent years, some climbers have told us strange stories. You know there are tales about a creature, who we call the Yeti. He comes from the old religion, before the Buddha taught us the Dharma, the way. We know that people from other parts of the world have their own stories about this Abominable Snowman that they weave into events that have occurred on the mountains. Maybe he is there... Or maybe you wish him to be there?' The boss paused, and the climbers nodded sagely. They were intrigued by the stories from the old times but, like the villagers, did not believe everything they had heard."

"Ooh," exclaimed Mary, "where's my bear?"

The man picked up a teddy bear from the foot of her bed and gave it to her. She cuddled it tightly and looked at him expectantly over its head.

"And what do you think the boss said then? Shall I tell you?"

"Yes, yes, Daddy!"

"The boss said, 'So, we can hire you some yaks—'"

"Yaks, yaks, yaks," said the two children together, having waited for this delightful word to appear. "Oh, tell us about the yaks, Daddy. Tell us about the yaks."

"Well, yaks are wonderful animals. They are very strong, and they have long fur and sharp horns, and they're good at walking on the mountain tracks and carrying heavy loads. They don't need much to eat – just vegetation – and they can eat ice and snow to get enough water. They give good milk as well, so the people in the village make cheese from it. The yaks provide them with what they need: milk, meat, fur for clothing, and dung for fertilising the fields."

"Too smelly – ugh!" said Mary, and the girls giggled. "How is it good for the fields, Daddy?"

"It's good because of all the natural chemicals that can be reused by the plants," explained Ellen seriously, suddenly a horticultural expert. "Isn't it, Daddy?"

"Yes, that's quite right, Ellen. The yaks are wonderful animals for these people. You can see how human beings can live in harmony with their animals in such an isolated place."

Their father's pontifications did not bother the children. "Go on, Daddy, go on. Where did they go with the yaks?" Their voices were sounding sleepier, and they settled back under the blankets, their faces peering out over the covers, teddy bears alongside them.

"So the climbers, with six porters from the village, set off on the track with four yaks. The first night, they camped in the forest on the hillside. There they heard unfamiliar sounds: local birds, rare frogs, distant and unearthly animal cries. The wind blew in gusts round them. They saw the moon floating through the treetops against the snow-capped mountains. They were captivated by the beauty of the place, but they were keen to get beyond the treeline to their base camp below the mountain. The base camp was high enough to be in perpetual snow, and although the men were concerned about staying in those very wintry conditions for too long, they were well prepared and knew that the porters were familiar with the territory and would help keep everything safe.

"The next day, they packed, loaded up the yaks, and headed further up the mountain. In no time, they were breathless. The air thinned as they reached about 5,000 metres, and they passed the snow line first, and then the treeline. Now the landscape was craggy, mountainous, and covered in snow. The going was tough even though they hadn't yet reached the steepest ice-decked pathways, but the animals trekked slowly and easily with their rhythmic, rolling gait, and seemed unperturbed.

"That evening, they reached base camp, and everything was unloaded. The porters set out the camp and stayed for one night to help the climbers get ready for the days to come. Some equipment would be left at the base camp ready for their return, and the villagers and their yaks would meet them in about a week's time. It was always a good idea to stay a couple of days at the base camp to acclimatise to the thin atmosphere and to prepare the equipment needed for the more difficult climb ahead.

"In the morning the sun was shining and the peaks above them looked magnificent – sharply defined in the bright light. The climbers prepared to spend the day working on their equipment and planning their next moves. They bade farewell to the porters and the faithful yaks as they set off down the mountainside."

"Bye-bye, yaks," said Ellen sleepily, hugging her bear and sucking her thumb.

Mary's eyes were closed already. The story was delivering its aim, and now the man talked mainly to himself, which had a calming effect on him too. Just telling the tale out loud was cathartic.

"A day later, they headed further up the mountain passes, aiming for a spot that one of the climbers had been to before. This was on a level hillside that would now be covered in snow, but from there they would have a magnificent view over the valleys to the distant peaks. They would also be able to prepare for the next day's more strenuous climb. It was a tougher climb than they'd expected, and when they reached their intended camping place the sun was setting behind their mountain, but the peaks across the valley, a kilometre or more away, were bathed in bright sunlight. One of the climbers gazed through his binoculars at the caves on the sides of the snowy peaks. Suddenly, he stood stock-still, looking intensely through the binoculars. He had seen something, but he wasn't sure what it was. Something had moved on the mountainside. Something that looked almost human."

"Ooh, almost human," said Ellen, struggling to maintain consciousness.

"Round the fire that night, they discussed their plans for the next day. They hoped to ascend another four or five hundred metres to another camping place, but they were uncertain of that plan because the weather didn't look promising. In the Himalayas, it's not unusual for storms to blow in very rapidly, and that's why so many climbers perish on those peaks. They decided to wait until morning to make a decision about whether they would move on. The climber with the binoculars mentioned that he might have seen something unusual, but he was not sure enough to make much of it.

"During the night there was a heavy snowfall, and when they woke up in the morning the snow at the sides of their tents and on their gear outside was half a metre deep. It was actually very cosy in the tents once the sun was out. The air was surprisingly warm, and they were able to sweep the snow away, but they decided it wouldn't be a good day to proceed further up the mountain, and so they agreed to stay put for the day. That gave them the opportunity to explore the area round their camp, and they found a number of caves nearby, none of which looked as if they had been occupied in the recent past. They found some animal bones which could only have come from a very long time ago. At this altitude, no mammals could survive for long alone.

"As the sun began to set, the climbers prepared a meal, and at the suggestion of the climber with the binoculars they surveyed that area in the distance where he had seen the apparition. Sure enough, as the sun was going down, one of the climbers saw a movement. It was too far away to be sure what it was, but it looked as if a large animal was walking on its hind legs through the snow between some caves. It didn't look human. If it was a bear, it was an odd one: it seemed to have some kind of furry grey coat, but it didn't move like a bear. Whatever the creature was, it seemed to be looking at them as intently as they were looking at it. They talked about the so-called Yeti and what it might be."

"Is there really a Yeti, Daddy?" asked Mary, her eyes still closed. "I wish there was."

"Well," whispered the man conspiratorially, "let's see, shall we?"

"Maybe we don't know all the animals in the world," remarked Ellen, removing her thumb from her mouth momentarily to allow her to speak.

"No, I'm sure we don't."

22

Both of the children snuggled down again peacefully. Anticipating the story still to come, they were fighting sleep as hard as they could.

"The sun went down. The climbers crawled into their tents and slept soundly. At about four o'clock in the morning they heard the snowfall begin again. They lay awake for a while and chatted to each other within the two-man tents. The strange creature they believed they had seen had been perhaps a kilometre away, so it was unclear what it was. Could it have been the Yeti? The climbers were determined to find out more, and a little concerned about what the creature might be and whether there were any others nearby. Soon, though, they went back to sleep.

"At about six o'clock in the morning, well before it was light, one of the climbers thought he heard a cough outside, and wondered why one of his colleagues was up and about at that time. Maybe he just needed a pee, but it was usually good to hold off leaving the tent until the sun rose.

"Later that morning, the first to rise was the climber who had first spotted the mountain creature two nights before. He drew back the tent's inner door flap, undid the zip, looked outside, and there, clear as day in the shining sunlight, he saw large, bare footprints leading from the edge of the cliff up to the side of his tent and then back again."

*

This was where the man always concluded the story, and his children would respond with oohs and aahs. Then he could tell them that they could go to sleep now, because the creature – the Yeti – had gone away down the mountain and they were safe. That was far enough for a children's tale. But tonight the girls were already asleep. The man sat back, watching them breathe, and then he drew up the covers around each of them, turned off

23

the lamp, and stood for a minute or two by the door, thinking wistfully about that mountain journey.

The climbers had never fully understood what had happened that night, although they had discussed it endlessly. When the first to rise had opened the tent flap in the darkness, torch in hand, he had found himself gazing into the piercing eyes of a hideously distorted face. Lit by the torchlight, it had looked as terrified as he had felt. The face twisted and grunted; a hideous coughing sound that sounded like "*Huí qù*", or 'Go back' in traditional Chinese. The creature repeated the sound two or three times, but it hadn't been clear whether the grunts were a human language or not. Its breath smelt of meat. Its body seemed to be covered in long grey fur. Was it the Yeti? Or perhaps a mountain hermit in a fur coat who had ascended from the Chinese side of the range and didn't want any strangers nearby? Or a refugee from the Chinese Civil War, still surviving after nearly thirty years? But before the climber could call the others, the creature fled down the mountain, leaving its tracks for all to see.

That day, as they struck camp and began to ascend further, the weather improved, and within two days they reached the summit, planted their flags, and prepared to return. They never saw the creature again, either up close or with their binoculars, despite looking for it. They never resolved what they had seen and what they believed about the Yeti. The villagers believed in the Yeti as part of their ancient religion but the climber who had come face to face with the creature asked himself, why did we enlightened Westerners want to believe? Even for the most rational of us, perhaps there is some deep longing within our psyche that seeks out doorways to something beyond. As we run out of lost lands and tribes unknown to man, we adopt symbols to keep the search alive, looking for something we recognise as somewhat human but not exactly like ourselves. Hobbits, Bigfoot, the Yeti.

A face in the dark.

GRC, September 2022
Recalling a cold night in Hamilton, New Zealand, 1998

Everything's Better with an Undo Button

I HAD THOUGHT IT WAS GOING TO BE A NORMAL DAY.

It was about eleven in the morning; a Thursday. I had been gathering my thoughts in advance of a meeting with some investors that afternoon, and gazing out of my thirty-third-floor office window across Singapore's breathtaking Marina Bay, which is always good for inspiration. I was counting the trees alongside the extraordinary boat-shaped pool on the Sands Hotel's enormous roof terrace when I heard the door squeak loudly – I really must get that hinge fixed – and Yun Yee, my personal assistant, burst into the room.

"It Simon here. That Simon again. Outside. You want see him, or I tell him go way, *lah*?"

Some months back, I had told Yun Yee about the episode with Simon, when he had tried to convince me that he had friends in the ninth dimension who could teleport physical objects – namely pizza – via gravitational waves. There was still something unsettling about that incident, but I couldn't quite remember what it was. Simon was an old university acquaintance, and now a ventures consultant with the renowned firm of Armstrong Baker Mollis Trivet Watterson and Zogbi. Actually, my interest in our friendship was less to do with venture capitalism and more to do with a rather attractive girl in the firm's finance department, whose phone number he had promised to get for me but which never seemed to materialise. He was always trying to sell me the rights to some new technological gizmo, or seal complicated deals on the spot, and I'm just not that kind of entrepreneur. I need spreadsheets, forecasts, net present value, customs clearance documents, distribution agreements – that sort of thing. I'm not a 'brown envelope full of hundred-dollar notes' kind of operator. Just as well in Singapore, where brown envelope operations are somewhat frowned upon. Anyway, Yun Yee's suggestion turned out to be futile because Simon was hot on her heels, arm stretched out in greeting as he stepped around her and into my office.

"Hey, Mike, me old mate!" he began.

Yun Yee looked startled, as well she might, raised her eyebrows heavenward, and looked at me for instructions.

"Bring some coffee, would you?" I smiled resignedly and collapsed back into my voluminous grey leather chair as Simon advanced towards the mahogany desk, arm still outstretched for a handshake. I took the proffered hand without getting up. Maybe this was the day he would give me the phone number? I would definitely feel more pally if he did.

"Good morning, Simon. Have a seat." Unable to resist it, I gestured to the hard chairs in front of my desk – the ones I keep for *special* visitors. "I suppose you have some news from the ninth dimension?"

"No. Haven't heard much from them, I'm afraid. They weren't too pleased about the meeting when you backed off so decidedly."

I shifted uncomfortably in my chair. My mental block having suddenly lifted, I could now clearly remember the strange end to that meeting when my perceptions of reality had been challenged by blue pepperoni and some extraordinarily vivid mental imagery featuring that finance lady of my hoped-for acquaintance.

"But don't worry about that now," he continued. "This is something entirely different."

"I see," I said, immediately kicking myself. I knew Simon would take that as a cue to continue at length about his latest scheme.

"You're familiar with Milan Kundera, of course?"

"Well, yes, of course," I responded truthfully. I was familiar with the renowned Czech novelist, having read a number of his intriguing stories and found them both entertaining and profound. I particularly liked *The Unbearable Lightness of Being*.

"In *The Unbearable Lightness of Being*," Simon went on, "Kundera points out that since we only have one life, we can never know whether our decisions are good or bad as we can't compare their results with those of other decisions."

As it happened, I had studied that book at university, where Simon and I had briefly shared some digs, and I had written a rather brilliant – I thought – finals essay on that very point. So it struck me as quite odd that he had raised that paragraph out of the whole of the prolific writer's works. "Yes, that's a fair paraphrasing of what he said," I responded.

"But now, Mike, we can." He paused for dramatic effect, which was rather ruined by Yun Yee bringing in the coffee and noisily planting the tray on the desk in front of him. I took my usual Americano with a dash of milk.

Yun Yee placed an identical cup in front of Simon. "Sugar, *lah*?" she asked, lifting the cut-glass bowl; an heirloom from my mother.

"Yes, sweetie, any time you like. Your place or mine?" said Simon.

I winced. Yun Yee glared at him, banged the sugar bowl down on the desk, grabbed the tray and, with her hips swaying aggressively, walked out and slammed the creaky door.

"Oops," said Simon, not looking at all regretful. He took a small device out of his pocket; about the size of a big mobile phone. It looked seriously cool: smooth lines with a matt black finish, a couple of dials, and a recess in which there was a big blue button. He adjusted something and pressed the blue button.

I turned away towards the window, cringing with embarrassment at Simon's outrageous faux pas and irritation at his cheap trick with a fake device. Regaining my composure with deep breaths, I took in the view across the marina towards the petal shape of the ArtScience Museum. Then I heard a noise. Yun Yee was back in the room, asking the same question. My eyes swivelled. The door was still closed as it had been after, moments before, she had slammed it on her way out, to its protesting creaks.

"Sugar, *lah?*"

"Yes please, if that's OK," Simon replied, with no hint of a leer.

Yun Yee put the sugar bowl down gently on the desk and spooned two heaped teaspoons of the brown crystals into Simon's cup. She smiled broadly at us both. "Mike, you need anything more, *lah?*" she asked. "I like go for early lunch if you busy."

I considered for a moment. Clever Yun Yee had given me the perfect get-out. Nonetheless, my interest was piqued by what had just happened. "Yes, that's fine," I replied with a brief wave, keeping calm and carrying on. "See you later."

"Don' forget DBS meeting two clock," she reminded me.

"Yes, fine, it's in the programme."

Yun Yee left the room, opening and closing the door to the accompaniment of the usual squeaking of its hinges.

I stood up and stared out across the marina again, focusing for a second, before turning back to Simon, who was grinning smugly. "Simon. What in the name of all that's rational just happened?"

Simon launched into a low-key pitch. "The undo button," he said, placing the small black device with the big blue button in front of me on the desk. "Everything's better with an undo button!"

This was almost as weird as our previous meeting, although on that occasion the major weirdness had not occurred until the end. This was full on, in your face, two minutes in. It was more than I could take. I told Simon to "Stay where you bloody are", ran across the room, wrenched the door open (creating a massive screech), and was about to berate Yun Yee for playing jokes on me when I realised that she wasn't there. Nor was her handbag. Her computer monitor had switched to its screen saver – pretty pussycats, of course. I looked around at the big open office beyond the secretarial alcove. All seemed perfectly normal. I realised my mouth was gaping open and my heart was beating very fast. With my head spinning, I shuffled back into my office, shut the creaking door, and made it to my comfortable chair before saying anything more. I took a deep breath.

"Now, you're going to have to give me some kind of explanation." I tried to sound cool, but I knew that I had just witnessed the impossible. The kind of impossible that even Sherlock Holmes would have trouble eliminating. I consciously downplayed my emotions. "And I hope it doesn't involve Czech novelists or the ninth dimension."

"No, no: that was quantum electrodynamics – this is general relativity," Simon said apologetically, as if that were a distinction that would satisfy most normal people.

I remained silent, but I noticed that my heart was still beating rather fast, and I was gripping the arms of my chair uncomfortably tightly.

"Now, we all know the ideas behind relativity are correct—" he began.

"Because of GPS needing it to work accurately?" I cut in carefully, trying to demonstrate a modicum of attention and understanding.

"Of course, and because of the experimental verification of gravitational lensing around exoplanets."

"Of course," I said, and immediately realised that that was an even worse response than 'I see'. If I was going to make any sense of this mind-shattering experience, I would need the explanation from first principles.

"Now," he continued, fighting – but not hard enough – to hide the victorious grin that twitched at the corners of his mouth. We both knew he'd got me. I cursed myself for actually finding this quite gripping. "Think of space-time as a giant four-dimensional meat loaf."

That was not a good start. I don't like meat loaf at the best of times, except for Meat Loaf the singer. But if I hadn't seen the exchange with Yun Yee with my own eyes, I would have been pretty sure that Simon was bats, if not a messenger straight from hell.

"You see," he continued, crossing his legs to show how comfortable he was with all of this physics, "I expect you think of the laws of physics as being immutable, not changing at all with time."

That was scary in itself. I often said to customers who were demanding deliveries sooner than was logically possible, "So you want me to change the laws of physics for you?" What I had just seen had shocked me into wondering whether, if the laws of physics might actually change, tomorrow's client might just reply, "Yes."

Simon continued, "So imagine you slice the meat loaf and move a slice backward along the time axis, then you can undo what has just happened – but only locally, of course, and in this case, just as regards the lovely Yun Yee."

I had heard that Einstein, the father of relativity, had said in a letter something like 'time is an illusion', but taking pieces of it and moving them around was beyond my wit to grasp. Nonetheless, I had just seen it done in my own office. I was getting the distinct feeling, too, that I had seen all of this before – was it that old déjà vu again?

Simon was leaning forward, and I could sense the hard sell coming just around the bend, steam whistle blowing. "We live in a relational universe, Mike. Relationships between entities – and people are no different – precede the emergence of space and time. This is nothing new, you know: Leibniz caught on to it and then Einstein just carved it up a bit and it came out as general relativity."

"Uh-huh," I said, rather proud of myself for not saying 'Of course' or 'I see', because I quite clearly didn't. I didn't think Professor Einstein would have much liked to hear his thought processes characterised as 'carving it up a bit', but then, he wasn't around to do so. Or was he? Was there some universe in which he heard every remark made about him? Then it crossed my mind that Simon was obviously fantastically well read but hadn't the first clue about how to sell a business proposition. Why was that, I wondered? Was he really an alien from a distant star system, like Ford Prefect in *The Hitchhiker's Guide to the Galaxy*? All of this wide-ranging philosophical speculation was a bit unexpected for a Thursday morning in the office. We were normally talking about the margins on new models of air conditioner. I had the feeling that Simon was going to quote something really obscure next – Borges, maybe?

"Wasn't it Jorge Luis Borges," he continued, "who believed in 'an infinite series of times, in a dizzily growing, ever spreading network of diverging, converging and parallel times'?" His arm lunged poetically towards the expansive view outside the window.

Now, Borges was also a literary favourite of mine, and I could vaguely remember that quote from his story 'The Garden of Forking Paths', but it wasn't Borges's opinion about time; it was that of a character of his who was about to shoot someone in the belief that, in another parallel time, it wouldn't happen, so it was OK. I could imagine a judge having a bit of a tricky moment with that.

"But…but…" I sputtered, "how do you control it? Surely the whole universe hasn't just shifted to the rear by a few seconds?"

"No, no, of course not. It's just like pressing Ctrl+Z on your computer."

"Uh-huh," was about all I could manage as Simon continued with his mystifying explanation.

"It's the relations, Mike. You, me and your rather lovely secretary were involved in a momentary cosmic event. The relations generate the space-time perceptions by harnessing random numbers generated in real time due to the quantum fluctuations of the vacuum, so the undo button just cancels the last relational event in the perception continuum."

Consciously stopping myself from saying 'Aaarrrgh!', I knew it was time for me to respond. "Simon, come on. You can't expect me to take this at face value. You've got to show me again. How about I boil that kettle over there," I pointed to the corner cabinet, "and then you can unboil it with your undo button?"

"No, Mike. Surely you don't think relational energy shifts in the perception continuum come for free? No, no: the temporal vortex relativistic manifold requires an appreciable time to recharge for a second time displacement – and indeed part of the necessary research is how to minimise or eliminate the recharge time."

I nearly said 'I see', but I managed to swallow it in time. Simon's explanation sounded vaguely plausible but mighty convenient.

"I can't do another demo until tomorrow," he continued. "I mean, if you try to do a relationship-driven time displacement with a partially charged temporal vortex manifold, there's no knowing what might happen."

Well, I couldn't disagree there. I wasn't about to have any partially charged temporal vortex manifolds going off in my office – especially not on the thirty-third floor. Nevertheless, as my blood pressure gradually returned to normal, I had the germ of an idea that could be a win-win for both of us, as well as a jolly nice relational event in the perception continuum. "Look, Simon, I'm utterly impressed. Cosmically, even. Much more than I was with the pizza scheme. Well, well – relativistic manifold shifts in the perception continuum vortex thingy, indeed. So what are you asking me for? You said something about research into the recharging mechanism? Do you want me to feed this into my white goods business? Dress it up in a futuristic-looking device that you can hang on your fridge to stop meat going off?"

"Mike, I'm truly disappointed that you think I'm here to ask for money – no, no, no! I just wanted to share this with you as one of my tech-savvy friends. And, well, if you think it's a great idea, sure, maybe there's partnership potential in there somewhere."

This was not the 'hard sell' Simon I was used to. This was more a 'soft and sloppy sell with big wet kisses' kind of pitch. The hard-to-get come-on. But it really didn't work bloke to bloke. If Simon had been that girl in his finance department, whom I was still thinking about in the background, then the cool approach might have ignited more of my enthusiasm. Nevertheless, I could see big potential here, even if Simon pretended he didn't. I was right: Simon hadn't the first clue how to sell a deal.

"Hold on a minute, Simon," I said. Playing the cool card myself, I stepped around the mahogany desk and headed for the door. "Let me just make a quick call."

I walked casually out of my office, sat on Yun Yee's chair, and called the tax department. "Hi, Foo Li, what was that you were telling me about a new R&D tax break?"

The phone rattled with the staccato voice of our tax accountant.

"I see," I said, because now I truly did. Today was the deadline to get in an R&D grant proposal and we had failed, through busyness and general indolence, to find a good project to submit.

Foo Li explained that if we could show that we had paid out 20,000 Singapore dollars for starting a new project, it would automatically reduce our tax bill by that amount. Money for nothing, to quote Dire Straits – but no available ladies involved, unfortunately, and especially none from the finance department of Armstrong Baker Mollis Trivet Watterson and Zogbi.

Thanking Foo Li and returning the phone to its dock, I strolled back to my office, feeling a bit more normal. "You're not going to believe this, Simon," I began, "but our R&D boys would really like a slice of this."

"Oh, right, great… Great, Mike. You're a pal," said Simon, with the kind of enthusiasm I would have expected. I could see his next question forming on his lips. "How much, exactly?"

"Twenty grand," I responded instantly. It was an amount I could see would pay his rent and bar bills for the next three months if he was a bit circumspect with the champagne at business lunches.

Simon's eyebrows shot up to somewhere beyond the top of his head.

"And I can transfer it to your business account right now – if, and only if, this is an exclusive deal."

"Yes, of course. You're the only fish in this sea, mate!"

I should have been suspicious about that, but I let it go. After all, this wasn't going to cost me anything, and if it was true and not some sleight of hand, I would have first call on the most astonishing technology I had ever seen. I would be the King of Industry 4.0; the Fourth Industrial Revolution people were all talking about – well, some people.

Being a digitally literate kind of guy, I got out my smartphone and did an instant PayNow transfer to Simon's mobile number. I also took the precaution of photographing the device with the big blue button, and printed out a receipt from my computer, into which I embedded the picture. I typed in some mention of R&D and an 'exciting new opportunity in the field of control technology and exclusive rights to development and exploitation'. Simon signed it like a lamb.

"Well, thanks, Mike. This is great," he said, extracting his phone from his pocket and opening the calendar. "Shall we arrange to meet the week after next to work on a plan for the productisation? I'll be out of the country next week."

In retrospect, waiting a week or more to start planning the most extraordinary technology product in the history of the universe should have seemed a bit odd. But never mind. I was keener to shake his hand than I had been at the beginning of this bizarre meeting, and so I did so. Simon smiled, picked up the undo button device from my desk, and, with little more said, left the room and closed the door quietly behind him. Strangely, it didn't squeak. I thought I heard an exclamation of "Yes!" filter through the door. It was then that I realised that I had forgotten to ask him for the gorgeous accountant's phone number.

Simon's an odd cove, signing away his rights like that, I thought. I'm looking forward to the planning meeting, though – must call his office on Monday to confirm the time. I wonder where he's off to next week that's so important? Anyway, I can have some of the tech guys start considering what this is all about. Might read up a bit on Leibniz in the meantime.

*

Simon entered the lift as quickly as he could, before his fortunes had a chance to change. This was a dramatic reversal in his previous experiences with Mike, who was not normally one to make a quick decision. He fingered the metal box in his pocket – amazing what you could get made up for a few dollars in Chinatown.

The old man had nodded wisely at his request for a cool device that looked as if it could change time, like Ctrl+Z. "Ah, the undo button," he had said, nodding sagely. Clever chap. Done in two days.

As he emerged on the ground floor, Simon felt as light as air. After a smart foreign exchange deal for the twenty grand, he could now plan his escape to Europe quickly. Shame about the venture capitalists kicking him out, but never mind now. He made his way through the security turnstiles and looked across the great atrium plaza under the three towers of the Financial Centre building. He was feeling a bit peckish and, spotting the ABC Bakery – a favourite spot – decided on the spur of the moment to drop in for a quick lunch, breathe a deep sigh of relief, and relax briefly on his laurels.

He was surprised to see Yun Yee sitting just inside the restaurant, and reckoned this must be the continuation of his run of luck. Now he wouldn't have to creep back into Mike's building to settle up with her.

"Hi, Yun Yee," he began brightly. "Thanks so much, you have no idea what this means to me."

She looked at him coldly. "What you mean, *lah*?"

"Well, Mike was completely taken in and you played your part perfectly."

"You very rude man, you know, *lah*? Now-day, nobody speak to lady like that."

"Oh, yes...well, I'm sorry, but it was all part of the plan. I told you I was going to say something a bit gross, so Mike would do his usual woke cringing and focus his attention elsewhere, hoping the problem would disappear, like he does."

"I din' want upset him like that – I thought you just play joke for him laugh," Yun Yee replied, still with a bit of a snarl.

"Well, maybe this will make you feel better." Simon sat down and surreptitiously passed her a hundred-dollar note across the table, hidden by her empty plate.

Yun Yee looked a bit surprised and sheepish. "Why you give me, *lah*?"

"Well, it's what we agreed, isn't it: a hundred, to play a good joke on Mike? Isn't it enough now?"

"You are mad man, Simon. Bad man. I no help you any more." Unexpectedly, she shoved the money back towards him.

"No – I'm sorry if I've upset you, but you did the job so well. Mike was absolutely stunned when he turned round and you were back in the room. How you managed to come in with the door closed, I really don't know."

She looked quizzical for a moment, and then blinked as she began to get the idea. "Simon, I can't take no money from you, *lah*."

"But you came back into the office, just as I asked you to, to get Mike going."

She tossed her hair and leaned closer to him across the table as her mood lightened a bit. He leaned back a little, not sure where this conspiratorial almost-flirtatiousness had come from.

His mind was running off its rails trying to work out what she meant. She loosed off one of her special smiles, reserved only for silly men.

"I cross with you, Simon. So I stop our arrangement, *lah.*" Yun Yee paused, enjoying the look of total confusion on Simon's face. "I din' come back in."

GRC, October 2021

Death on the Rhine

AS HIS LUXURIOUS MERCEDES E-CLASS TAXI DREW UP outside the Hotel Schloss Reinhartshausen on the bank of the Rhine an hour or so west of Frankfurt, James Major looked up at the magnificent building. It was nearly 700 years old. In the setting sun, its white walls glowed pink. The stunning location never failed to impress. Major ran a hand through his thinning fair hair and smoothed his small moustache. His visit to the barber that morning had been worthwhile: he was determined to impress too. He felt confident that the meeting at the Schloss could be an opportunity to advance his reputation among his colleagues, and in particular in the eyes of Dieter Halbstadt, the quiet but effective chief executive officer of the corporation.

Major reached inside his grey Yves Saint Laurent suit jacket, lined with red silk, and extracted his wallet to pay the driver. Despite his thirty-eight years, his face was still a little prone to acne. And, despite his senior position in a large multinational corporation, he was still an occasional victim of loneliness and its companion evils of self-pity and the consumption of too much brandy.

As he wheeled his minimalist suitcase into the hotel's foyer, Major hummed to himself. He enjoyed getting away from the office, and would always feel a little frisson of excitement on arriving at a smart hotel. An elegant dinner or two was on the cards, and prior to that, a meeting at which he could sit back, let others do most of the work, and pipe up with an occasional well-timed and astute comment that would make everyone realise why he was where he was today: at the top, or at least as near the top as he cared to be right now. Of course, he knew that being *too* near the top was an invitation to those who followed the prophet Machiavelli to terminate his comfortable corporate existence. Nevertheless, such fears were far from his mind as he checked in and went up to his room. As the bellboy showed him the facilities, Major had a fleeting desire to press a ten-euro note into his hand and ask if a friendly lady could be found later. But no – this was a reputable establishment and he was a respectable (if still reasonably attractive) man. One who recognised that loneliness is a hard master and compels one in strange ways.

*

In the morning, during a decent buffet breakfast, and while Major was mingling with the assembled executives from all over Europe, he noticed a rather striking middle-aged lady who he guessed must be the new commercial advisor. She had been mentioned a couple of days ago in a note confirming the agenda for the conference. The note had explained that she had recently sold her successful retail business in Italy for a substantial sum and had been retained as a catalyst for the company's commercial planning. Major had not had the chance to ask the CEO about this person or what she was expected to accomplish. Nonetheless, he was used to consultants, whose advice could be absorbed and exploited if it aligned with his own thinking and ignored if it did not. Most were clever but inexperienced. This one was experienced, but was she clever? Let's hope not too clever, Major thought to himself, feeling a slight discomfort.

The meeting began well enough. Major was on the top table, although not in the chair. He was happy with this. It meant less effort; yet he could still bask in the approval of the audience of some fifty executives. One who had made it and was up there to be admired and emulated. During the first presentation – a project progress report – he gazed around the room, appreciating the decor. Good finishing was so important. His notes were assiduous – or, rather, he made it look as if they were. He glanced at the medieval portraits in their gold-leaf frames. His moment would come later when he presented the strategic plan for the next year. This was what he was good at: leading from the front, inspiring people with a mission, and then sitting back and watching them carry it out. He was a general, not a sergeant major.

In the coffee break, he girded his loins and networked a bit more seriously. There were some favours he wanted to call in, to ensure support for one or two of his more provocative proposals. He was friendly with the team – not superior, but knowing. People tried to get near him; to get his ear. Old-timers wanting to influence The Plan. New guys, fresh-faced and keen to impress. And he wanted to get a couple of minutes with Halbstadt, the chief exec: cool and distant, but authoritative. As inscrutable as a piece of furniture.

"This afternoon, I want you to be making clear," the CEO said firmly in his good but less-than-perfect English, "that we will not the easy time be having in the next twelve months."

Major looked up at the taller man and nodded sagely.

"You have the figures been seeing," continued Halbstadt. "We are looking at the difference between the two large numbers: the revenue and the costs. A small percentage – say, two per cent this way or that way – means the gravy with the wurst or down the river going."

This was not news, and Major's plans could handle the risks. Nonetheless, doubt touched his features as he agreed. The danger would be the new commercial advisor. He asked Halbstadt to explain a bit more about her role, and why she had been hired without the top team being consulted, which was unusual.

Halbstadt was evasive. "You see, this lady a very successful career has been having. She much profit from selling her business in Italy has made. I think she can add the something – the shininess, shall we say – to our thinking. For the tactics. You know? How we the things do that we do."

Major did not quite see what part shininess could play in corporate success. Perhaps he meant brilliance? Nevertheless, he nodded, wishing to appear satisfied with the answer, and then Halbstadt excused himself and moved on to another knot of coffee drinkers.

Peering across the throng, Major spotted the Italian lady again on the other side of the large room. Wanting to get some measure of her, his instant impression was that she was in her late fifties, elegant, not especially attractive, no longer slim, flamboyantly dressed, edgy, and opinionated. He could see that even at long range, as she was wagging her finger to make a point. He was certain that she would be out to make an impact today. Only yesterday, the CEO had insisted that the figures Major had prepared should be sent to her for information purposes, and Major had reluctantly agreed. However, the figures she had been sent were not the final set. Knowing the business so much better than any new advisor, Major had added some flourishes of his own. He was a risk-taker. Calculated risks, of course. Risks which in the good times nearly always paid off. Managing the bad times was a less common experience. He strolled back from the coffee room, chatting briefly to a few others, and made his way to the rostrum with a second coffee in hand. He noted that the Italian lady was already there, seated next to Halbstadt, who was listening intently to her.

Halbstadt stood up as Major sat down. "Now, ladies and gentlemans, I wish to introduce for you our new advisor of the commercial, who will explain some of the new methods we for the budget controlling will be using. So please for welcome the Frau Ortensia Lombardi."

The lady rose rapidly to her feet. Her long red dress had a deep side slit and was dotted with small black spots. To Major it seemed a little low-cut for business wear. She looked impressive, as she no doubt intended to, and despite her substantial frame she moved elegantly across the podium. Major noticed a slight hesitation in her stride, which disappeared the minute she stepped behind the lectern and drew a long breath. Her presentation was spectacular. She gesticulated at the screen, coming up with unexpected twists. She presented only five slides, each of which contained few words but many exclamation marks. She could make zero-based budgeting, traffic light analysis and monthly flash reports sound like a rock show in a high-stakes casino.

"In my experience, which is considerable," she declared, seeming to flow about the stage in front of the top table, caressing the microphone and gesturing expansively, "most corporate planning is a waste of time in a downturn. A. Waste. Of. Time," she repeated slowly and firmly, as if admonishing a child. "So you have to do what you can to make the most of your assets. Anything more than that is not a practical proposition." Her English was accented but flawless, and the Mediterranean style of it made her words salty with authority. "You must rely on the people – the good people – to get you through. You need to know who the good people are."

As she sat down with a flourish, flicking her red skirt over her knees, Major thought she glanced at him smugly. From the audience, all of whom presumed that they were among the 'good people' she had commended, there was enthusiastic applause.

Major was concerned but not worried, and lunch went well. He was always on form over a good meal, and the meal was very good. The Schloss could really turn it on. It was a wine producer as well as a hotel and restaurant, and the cellar visit scheduled for the evening was always one of the highlights of any stay there. Wine flowed sparingly over lunch, and Major was particularly careful. He could see that the Signora had laid down a challenge for him, and he was rising to it nicely over the fruit salad. On the way back to the auditorium, he saw her come out of the lift with Halbstadt. They seemed to be having another animated conversation. She was holding on to his arm, as if for support.

The graveyard slot at two o'clock was Major's. Not a problem for an accomplished public speaker, as he was.

Halbstadt introduced him in his inimitable style. "And now I am most pleased to bring for you Herr James Major, who will the success of our future for us explain."

The audience was sleepy, and Major woke them up with a couple of jokes about strategic planning – not an easy task. He was not at all complacent with this audience. They were sharp and not as susceptible as an American board to slides in four colours projected ten feet high. They would question and they would discuss. Nothing could be taken for granted. They interrupted and they debated, but he rolled with the blows and after the first half-hour he had them in his hands. He had proposed two strategic initiatives: moving into parts of the Middle East, and withdrawing certain products from countries in Western Europe where the competition and cost base were not satisfactory. The discussion was positive and even the country heads affected were in general agreement – having, of course, been lobbied first.

All went well until he came to the figures. Major could see Signora Lombardi pricking up her ears as he displayed the first financial slide. Here was one of his flourishes: a suggestion that accounting departments could be amalgamated over the Eastern European sector, saving about fifty staff. Halbstadt looked pleased. Lombardi looked as if she had just been handed a juicy steak. She stood up to ask a question – or more to deliver a lecture, as it turned out – and it was at that point that Nancy

Miles walked into the room and sat down at the back. Nancy was not so much an old flame of Major's as an unlit match, and he had not been expecting to see her at this meeting. Her appearance gave him a glow of pleasure, but meant that he missed the drift of Signora Lombardi's question.

"I'm sorry, could you say that again, Ortensia?"

"It was perfectly clear. I was just pointing out that in a downturn we will need to manage our finances in the region very…positively. So I believe it is self-evident that your suggestion is unwise. Indeed, foolish."

In Europe, business is usually polite. To be called a fool during your presentation is really not on. However, Major was not a man to be easily thrown or provoked. "Well, before coming to any premature judgement," he continued politely, not letting his irritation surface, "let me show you the remaining figures and then we can discuss them on the basis of complete information." He was pleased to have carefully avoided the word 'ignorant'. Fifteen all.

The figures were duly presented and showed a most pleasing upturn in profit against a downturn in revenue. Major thought he had steered a fair course through some choppy waters. He was about to sit down and take questions when the now condescending voice of Signora Lombardi broke in.

"Well, Mr Major," she said mellifluously, leaving her seat, striding across the podium towards Major standing at the lectern, and avoiding the first-name terms which were usual in the organisation. Halfway to reaching him, she came to a sudden halt and leaned heavily on the table; a flash of discomfort troubling her features. "You have given us a perfect example of what I said earlier: corporate planning is *a waste of time* in a downturn."

A swell of muttering rose among the audience, but died away quickly.

Signora Lombardi strode over to the screen and began stabbing a finger at one or two of the numbers. "If you reduce the financial administration, then this unit and," she stretched upwards, revealing black lace edging under her red dress, "that department will have to do their own variance analysis for the monthly flash reports. This will require four extra people to meet my targets. Staff who will not have a job for the rest of the month."

This level of tactical detail was not the sort of thing Major wanted to hear in a strategic planning discussion, but a quick glance at the audience showed that the country heads involved were nodding. Bad news. At the back of the room, Nancy crossed her legs and looked at the floor.

Halbstadt intervened. "I think, Ortensia, that James will of this problem have been recognising – haven't you, James?" He smiled at Major; it appeared genuine.

Major busked. "Ah, yes, of course. I was anticipating that any additional workload could be managed by a couple of extra days' effort from our accountants in those countries, operating as a team. They're familiar with our books, very bright, and could handle it quickly." Thirty all.

"And expensively," said Signora Lombardi, looking down her nose like a cobra about to strike – unpredictable and dangerous. "I think you will see that four days per month across ten territories over the year is going to outweigh any saving made by cutting the finance department."

Nancy looked up and caught Major's eye, but did not smile.

Major was getting rattled. This was a spurious argument based on unsupported assumptions about workloads and capacity, but to say so at this point would be out of place in a strategic discussion. As soon as debate was reduced to the level of talking about individual salaries, the whole vision thing went out of the window. He wanted them to concentrate on the big picture. "Ortensia, I think we should leave the detail people to sort out the finer points. Let's focus on the direction of the company. Think about where we want to be in five years. Not just this temporary market setback, which all of our competitors are facing as well."

"Mr Major, are you aware of our level of debt compared to our main competitors in Europe? Any one of them is better placed to take on the Middle Eastern market than we are."

That was not a financial issue, but a strategic one. Major began to feel like a general who was going to have to resort to rhetoric rather than logic to urge his troops forward. "It's not a matter of debt. It's a matter of targeted investment and profitability," he responded, a little too loudly.

"Herr Halbstadt, we will speak about this over dinner. Your Mr Major does not have the right approach," said Signora Lombardi, letting Major off the hook for the moment with a flea in his ear, like a schoolboy being threatened with the headmaster's office.

Major recognised that she had game point now and didn't want to waste it during the tea break.

The session ended lamely, with Halbstadt thanking Major briefly and not asking for any more questions. Could this be the moment at which Major's career died a painful death? He felt both furious and chastened for having been so badly prepared for these criticisms. He couldn't recall ever having been spoken to like that in his entire professional life.

He headed straight for Nancy. "Didn't expect to see you here. I mean, great to see you. Did you hear what that woman said? She made me look an idiot."

Nancy was cool – a production engineer by trade, and not prone to unconsidered judgements. Taking a Cambridge engineering degree as a beautiful woman outnumbered fifteen to one by large, hairy men had given her a sound training in handling herself in emotional situations. "Let's say, she has her own agenda."

"Yes, clearly," Major responded, not sure at all what that agenda might be. "I'll wait until the wine tasting tonight and see if I can talk informally to her. She may not be as rough-tough as she looks."

At last Nancy smiled, and Major felt a lot more comfortable. He suddenly realised that he had not seen the redoubtable Signora Lombardi smile at all. If anything, between speeches, she had looked a little pained.

*

At half past five, an hour after the meeting finished (which gave the delegates a chance to answer some of their messages, get changed and brush up), the group walked slowly down the winding half-kilometre road from the hotel to the winery. Major had latched on to Nancy and they were chatting comfortably. Walking together about five metres ahead were Halbstadt and Signora Lombardi. Major had his eye on them both. He was a little surprised that the Italian lady was holding on firmly to Halbstadt's arm; not seemingly in any gesture of intimacy but because – despite her energetic performance in the afternoon – she was having some trouble walking the distance.

Major remarked on it to Nancy. "Do you think our Ortensia is having some trouble with her legs?" he asked.

"You haven't done your homework, have you, James?" replied Nancy, somewhat to Major's surprise. "I thought you would have checked up on her as soon as that note came out from the secretariat to say she would be here."

"Well, no. As a matter of fact, I didn't have a chance to google her. The link that Halbstadt's secretary sent with the note was just a press release about her selling her retail business. I didn't get the chance to look further."

"Getting sloppy in your old age, James." Nancy gave him a friendly punch on the arm. "I suggest you do. The rumour is that she sold the company because she's very ill. She's close to Dieter Halbstadt, you know, but I guess you can see that."

"Tell me more." Major was a little alarmed that he had missed something important.

"There isn't much to tell, although I'm planning to check it out further. Whatever the health problem is, she's keeping it to herself. What seems to happen is that she can put on a show like she did this afternoon, and then she becomes exhausted and has to recover. Probably has some medication to give her a boost. I'm not sure she'll make the dinner tonight, but she wasn't going to miss the wine tasting."

"Why the wine tasting?" asked Major.

"She's well known in Italy as a wine connoisseur. Gets interviewed by the press about wines. She had a great range in her stores. In fact, she started out as a wine buyer."

"Well, I'm certainly going to do some googling now. Thanks for the heads-up," he said as they reached the door of the winery and transitioned from the balmy late afternoon to the dark, cool, refreshing atmosphere of the wood-lined wine cellar.

Halbstadt introduced the session, saying a few words about team building, the pleasures of the grape, and the relationship between the two. He introduced Signora Lombardi again, this time not as a corporate catalyst, but as a wine expert. She spoke seriously and enthusiastically about the wines of the Schloss, and explained the particular qualities of each wine selected for the event. As the tasting went on, the noise in the ancient building intensified; the Signora providing an animated and fascinating commentary on the wines being circulated among the group. Even Major was quite absorbed by the cheerful atmosphere and the camaraderie being generated. After half an hour or so the speech-making was over, and the cellar master took the floor and explained that they would now be given a short tour of the winery.

Halbstadt continued to hold Signora Lombardi's arm as the convivial crocodile of executives moved off into the cavernous darkness of the cellar. Meanwhile, Major felt Nancy's hand brush his, ever so slightly. She smiled warmly at him.

*

The dinner did not go as planned. The dining room was crowded and Major managed to find his way to Halbstadt's end of the top table. Mysteriously, and as hinted at by Nancy, Signora Lombardi was not there. Major enquired as to why.

"Ah, James," Halbstadt replied, "I am afraid the Signora is not so well feeling, and rest is wishing."

"I'm sorry to hear that. I was hoping for a lively debate over dinner."

"I too am sorry also not the debate to be having. Ortensia, you know, is for me an old…friend, and a very successful businesswoman being. She has some good ideas – maybe a little unusual. You can learn from her much, I think."

That did not sound good, thought Major. His relationship with Halbstadt had always been a little distant, a little formal, but he had put that down to their different business cultures and Halbstadt's unique style of expressing things in English. Now he wondered if maybe there was something more sinister in Halbstadt's remark. "Well, I am always keen to learn," he responded.

"Yes, of course," replied Halbstadt, smiling broadly. "You have always the quick learner been." He patted Major on the shoulder as they sat down.

It was the asparagus season in mid-April – *spargelzeit* – and the meal was magnificent. The region's white asparagus was truly delicious, and on this occasion was served with a hollandaise sauce, boiled new potatoes, and ham. After the first mouthful, Major was seriously impressed. The more he savoured the meal, the better it tasted. One of the best meals he had had in his life, perhaps. And the Rheingau Riesling from the Schloss's own collection complemented it perfectly.

He exchanged brief remarks with Halbstadt, who agreed that the meal was excellent, but the CEO was disappointingly preoccupied with his other neighbour. For Major, the pleasure of the meal was overshadowed by his concern about the Signora's influence on Halbstadt, although his mood was lightened by the remembrance of Nancy's smile at the winery.

So at the end of the meal, he went in search of Nancy, who he thought would at least be good company. He found her in a group of coffee drinkers standing around a tall table by the windows overlooking the river about twenty metres away. In his position, it was easy for him to join the group and the conversation they were having around some technical matter.

Then one of the finance guys changed the subject. "James, I think you're right about reducing the local finance groups, but Ortensia had a point today about the flash reports. They're a really good method to keep us on track month to month. I should think there's a way you two could come to a shared view on that?"

Major hadn't joined the discussion to talk about flash reports, but to inveigle Nancy away for a quiet chat. Nonetheless, for a few minutes he joined in a spirited exchange of views, so as to seem genial and flexible as regards the Signora's points. After a polite interval he managed to lead Nancy away, claiming a desire to take in the fresh air by the river. She agreed and followed him, while the others continued their financial debate.

*

Nancy and Major walked down to the towpath at the riverbank. It was close to 8.30 and the sun was setting, leaving the river glistening in the twilight. They walked for a while to the west, watching a few big barges drift lazily by on their way upriver. They talked about the company, about the wine tasting, and about the quality of the meal, which both agreed was outstanding.

"Did you enjoy the Riesling?" asked Major.

"Well, I only had a glass – you know me: I don't like to drink too much at these gatherings. The men get enough ideas without me being over-relaxed as well."

"Not many ladies here this time."

"No. Not many invited, it seems. I was wondering whether the Signora doesn't like too much competition around." Nancy smiled mischievously.

"Judging by her performance today, she could flatten any competition at a glance," said Major, his soreness at the afternoon's takedown still much in mind.

"It looks like an act to me," Nancy surmised. "More form than substance, you know. I often wonder how people like that become so successful."

"Yes. I've seen quite a few like that over the years. Charisma seems to trump analysis every time, but people like her usually have some strong technical background that they can lean on."

"Technology changes, though," mused Nancy. "I don't think she would risk getting into a technical argument, even about finance. She'll stop at common sense and putting one over on someone she thinks she can beat in an argument."

"I never got the chance to argue," said Major, shaking his head disappointedly. "Dieter stopped the conversation before I could respond."

"Just as well, I would say. From what I overheard, she's formidable in the crossfire and will go for the man if she fails to defeat his arguments. She could just abuse you and – believe me, James – you wouldn't know where to put yourself."

"Yes, I know what you mean," said Major with a worried frown. "Defending myself against personal attacks is not my forte. And in this kind of business, it's just grossly indecent to have a personal slanging match at a meeting. I would have had to just shut up and take it."

"You're right," Nancy agreed. "Look, it's getting a bit chilly. Let's go back."

They turned back down the path; Major a little disappointed that nothing remotely romantic had happened. Then Nancy stopped and gazed at the darkening river again.

"Are you OK?" said Major, moving close beside her in the hope of another touch of hands that could be taken further.

"Yes, it's nothing. I don't think the illness is an act, though. From what I've seen today and what I've read, she could be quite seriously adrift healthwise."

"Maybe too much emotion, too much pressure?" suggested Major.

"And let's not forget, too much wine."

"She didn't seem at all tipsy, even though she was knocking it back tonight."

"No, but did you see that Dieter got a car for her to go back to the Schloss after the tour?"

Major wanted to say, 'No, I was thinking about your smile.' Could he say that? Here and now? And would it be a dreadful turn-off? "No, I was thinking about your smile," he said.

He thought he saw a moistening of her eyes. She smiled again and looked at him.

"You flatter me," she managed to say, before turning away again.

They continued walking back in silence. As they crossed the hotel lobby towards the lifts, they noticed Halbstadt and Signora Lombardi talking together in an alcove.

"She looks tired," said Nancy, looking at Major with a concerned frown. "There's something not quite right about her skin: it's kind of waxy."

The lift arrived and they got in. Nancy's room was on the second floor; Major's on the third. The lift stopped at the second floor.

"Well, goodnight," she said. And, after a moment's silence, looking at the floor, "Thanks for the walk and the chat. It really is good to see you again, James." She touched him on the shoulder and stepped out of the lift.

Before he could stop himself, Major added a coda. "You know where I am if you want me." He smiled and tried to avoid any kind of leer.

Nancy laughed out loud and waved goodnight.

*

The knock on the door came about an hour later. Major looked up from his hotel-room desk, where – against his better judgement – he was trying to see if he could harmonise the Signora's views concerning the Middle Eastern market with his own. He still

57

hadn't made time to google her. He noticed his heart beating fast – could it be that Nancy had decided to make a bit more of the opportunity than he had really been expecting? He would welcome it. He opened the door.

"I'm sorry to bother you, Mr Major," Ortensia Lombardi began. "May I come in for a moment?"

Surprised as he was, Major stepped to one side, opened the door and invited her into his room. She moved slowly, with a stick. A pale shadow of the afternoon's fiery harridan.

"Please take a seat." He pointed to the comfortable sofa and armchairs under the windows of the big suite. "Can I get you a drink?"

"No, no. I don't need more after the tasting," she said brightly. But as Nancy had observed earlier, she looked tired. And more than tired, she looked unwell – pasty under her heavy make-up – and she was breathing rather heavily. "I… I want to apologise," she said unexpectedly, and a little awkwardly. "I was a bit over the top this afternoon in what I said to you…about you. You were right about our competitors. If we invest in a focused way, we have the resources. I've checked that."

"Well," responded Major, considerably taken aback, "I appreciate your saying that. You know it's not normal to be contradicted so directly in that kind of meeting. It felt a bit personal."

"Yes, yes. My apologies. I must confess that in a situation like that, I tend to play-act a bit. I'm used to having to put down some uppity people in my company…my old company. Some who really don't have their facts mustered. But I believe – now – that you do."

Could that have been Halbstadt's doing, Major wondered? If it was, it was more than good of him. Maybe Major's career wasn't dead after all.

"Dieter is a very good man, you see," Ortensia continued. "I've known him a long time. Once…"

"Go on," Major encouraged her.

"Once, maybe, I loved him. Maybe I…" She stopped.

That was quite a confession. Halbstadt was so focused, and so wrapped up in the business and in pleasing the shareholders, it was hard to imagine him having the energy to love anyone, or even to be loved.

"So, what do you say?" she continued. "Can we be friends? Allies to help poor Dieter get through?"

"Yes, I'm a great supporter of Dieter. He's a good leader – good judgement, flexible, strong intellect. But what has he got to get through?"

"The death of his wife, of course," she said with a note of surprise. "You didn't know?"

Major shook his head, shocked. "No. I didn't even know he was married. He's a very private person. But I feel remiss that I didn't know he was going through such a bereavement right now."

"Yes. And it's harder for him because it was here that she died."

Major looked at her, startled. He gestured around the room. "Here? At the Schloss?"

"Yes. She had been sick for over a year – brain cancer – and she asked him to bring her here one last time. They had their honeymoon here, you know. She loved it. She had a bed set up to look out over the river – quite beautiful. She was very happy for her last days."

"I have to confess, I'm shocked," said Major quietly. "Really surprised. No one in the company seems to know – it hasn't been mentioned at all." Not even Nancy knew, he thought to himself.

"He does keep his private affairs very quiet, I know. It's one of his strategies to give him strength for leading this show. I think that's why he wanted me to come this week: he needs to lean on me. I don't mind that at all." Ortensia's eyes were glittering. "But he can't do that forever, and that's why I want us to be allies."

"Well, I'm glad he has you as an old friend, and of course I'll support him. Does he know you're telling me this?"

"Yes. I asked him tonight. He trusts you. And so do I."

Major was buoyed by this show of confidence from a woman who only a few hours ago had seemed to be hellbent on wrecking his career. "So, what you said this afternoon – it was a kind of show of strength for him?"

"Yes, I was acting. I am a good actor, no?" A slight Italianism crept into her perfect *Inglese*. "But I am also a sick woman. I'm sure you have noticed. And your friend – the lady – she is very sharp. I think she sees everything."

Major was baffled but very relieved at this turn of events, despite his growing concern for Dieter Halbstadt and his situation.

"Now, I must leave you to your calculations." Ortensia tried to stand up from the low sofa. "You'll have to help me, I'm afraid."

Major helped her to her feet and passed her her stick, which had fallen down beside the sofa. She held his arm as they walked the few metres to the door. She really was breathing heavily.

"Are you OK getting to your room?" he asked.

"Yes. I'm OK. It's the same floor, just round the corner." She stepped out into the corridor and turned to him. "Thank you for your understanding. It's the medication I have to take that makes me aggressive sometimes. But it's also my worry for poor Dieter. Thank you for being there for him."

"I appreciate you coming to see me."

"You are a young man. A clever young man. There are many adventures ahead for you…" She stopped, gazed up the corridor for a moment, and continued with a broad smile, "But the lady – she will not come tonight!"

Then Ortensia set off at a surprising pace down the corridor, leaning heavily on her stick. Major got some sense of how beautiful she must have been when she was his age, and how she had worn herself away running a business even bigger than the corporation. He watched until she rounded the end of the passage, then stepped back inside his room.

*

In the morning, Major came down a little late to breakfast, having handled a few urgent emails first. There was a strange atmosphere in the crowded room. A quietness. Neither Halbstadt nor Ortensia was in evidence.

Nancy saw him and came over as he was collecting some bacon and hash browns at the buffet. "Let's sit down," she said firmly.

They sat together at an otherwise empty table with some used cutlery and crockery still to be collected.

"She's gone," said Nancy decisively.

"Gone? Who's gone? Gone where?" Major feared he had been wrong-footed again. What had he missed?

"Ortensia. Dieter went to wake her this morning when she hadn't come down. He found her on the bed, fully clothed. Dead."

Major stood, and his breakfast plate clattered to the floor. "But that's impossible. She came to see me. I thought it might be you," he added quietly. "She told me a story about Dieter and his wife."

Nancy looked a bit surprised. "Yes? You still haven't got it, have you?" she said, looking up at him quizzically.

"What? Not more mysteries?" Slowly, he sat down again.

"She *is* his wife."

Major realised that his mouth was hanging open. "She came to see me, ten o'clock or so last night, and asked me to 'help Dieter through it'."

"Through what?" enquired Nancy.

"She said to help him through…the death of his wife." Major was flabbergasted. He couldn't get his head around these bizarre events. Too much death: his career, Ortensia, Dieter's wife. Were they all the same? And in this lovely place, it seemed impossible to grasp.

"Anyway, the conference is going to conclude this morning," Nancy stated. "Dieter said he can't carry on until all this is sorted out. He said he would call you. So make sure your phone – your *Handy*, as Dieter calls it – is on."

Major got the mobile out of his pocket and saw a missed call from Halbstadt. He switched the ringer on and called him back. Nancy, meanwhile, had put her hand on his shoulder and was leaning close to him. The phone rang and was quickly answered.

"Dieter, I had no idea—" Major began.

"James. It's OK. I have…secrets." Halbstadt sounded sad, but in control as always. "I cannot to the conference come back. Maybe never I can to that beautiful place go more. Please, take over the chair. I know you can see the morning through. And break the conference at lunchtime. The colleagues in the afternoon can go home. Please tell them I am sorry their time to waste, but I know you can take charge."

"Yes, of course, Dieter. I am here for you. Really, I am."

"On you I rely. I know my trust is in you well placed. Acting CEO for a while you will be. Maybe for a long while. For you with the decisions I will be trusting. Out of the country for a time must I go. To Italy. So much she could have done."

"I am very sorry for your loss, Dieter. And I will do everything to make sure the company runs smoothly while you're away."

"I know you will." The phone went dead.

*

It was little problem to Major to chair a small number of technical sessions and declare the conference closed at lunchtime. His confidence returned, but he was haunted by the events of the previous evening. He could not understand what had happened. Had Ortensia's visit to his suite been some kind of apparition? She had seemed solid enough. But the outcome was marvellous for him. He was now CEO for the foreseeable future, but he had lost out on the experience that Dieter and Ortensia working together could have brought to the next steps in the company's journey. Key man risk was a real thing. If you depended on one person for your company to flourish, then one day it was destined to fail. For the sake of both of them, he would not let that happen.

Most of the delegates skipped lunch and left for the airport. Nancy and Major dined together with a few stragglers trying to impress the new acting CEO.

When coffee was finished, it was Nancy who suggested that they go out and walk by the river to try to take in the momentous events. They walked to the west again. It was cool but comfortable, and the river traffic was much busier than it had been the previous evening. Their hands brushed, and in a decisive moment Major took hold of hers. She squeezed his hand in return.

"I can't believe we were here on this path a few hours ago, wondering if my career was dead because of Ortensia. Now she is dead, Dieter is gone, and I am left holding the monkey," Major said, but his facial expression was contented. "Why did she come to see me like that after the altercations of the afternoon?"

"Don't underestimate the healing power of completion," said Nancy thoughtfully, and looked up at him with a smile. "She couldn't leave you hanging out to dry when you were her and Dieter's only hope of keeping the show on the road. She must have known that the end was upon her."

"Wise words."

They walked on in silence as a huge Dutch barge sailed by; its wake caressing the shoreline and washing over the grass on the lower banks.

"You know what I think is the saddest thing?" Nancy asked.

"Go on."

"All that skill. All that knowledge. Just gone in an instant."

"Yes, I see what you mean. She could have helped us so much once the emotions had calmed down. It's the tragedy of humankind. We can write things down, publish management books, run training courses, but it's those who have actually done the job who have the surest touch."

"And judging by what she made from selling her business, she certainly knew what she was doing, despite the performance art!" Nancy smiled at him. "But does it all go? Just like that? Even the memory of someone offers *some* help, doesn't it? I like to believe that maybe something is freed in death, so that the content of a life is able to find its way into the material of the universe, and we're all enriched by it in the end."

"That's a very romantic notion – with a capital R," Major mused, slowing for a moment, intrigued by the thought. "If I could absorb some of Ortensia's skills from the ether, it might make things a bit easier for me now." He tried to sound worried, but his calm smile gave away his happiness at being in the driving seat. "I'm going to need a lot of help, you know."

Nancy squeezed his hand again. "Well, maybe you need some help in other directions too."

They walked on in companionable silence, knowing that everything had changed.

GRC, January 2023

A Glitch in the Fabric of Space-Time

"Seven minutes late! Don't think I haven't been watching you! You've been working here for a month and you're always seven minutes late. What the hell is wrong with you? This is an operational business. You're here to man the phones. Someone in distress could be calling and you're not there to answer.

How does that make us look, eh? How does it make us look?"

"I'm sorry, Mr Meadows, really I am," stammered Ronnie. "I set my alarm, but I never seem to have enough time."

"You only live half a mile away, for God's sake," Meadows roared, throwing his great bear arms into the air. "Just bloody well get here by nine. Don't let me have to tell you about this again. Treat this as an official warning. Now get in there and get on with your job."

"Yes, Mr Meadows. I'm sorry, really I am. I don't know why—"

Meadows was already walking away, his huge shoulders straining against the starched white shirt he habitually wore. "Out of my sight... Now." He waved his arm towards the ops-room entrance.

Ronnie opened the door to the ops room. Everyone was in their cubicles, heads down, talking to customers. There was a buzz of concentrated conversation, so no one noticed him come in. He slumped into his chair, feeling deeply ashamed and incredulous that yet again he had failed to get to the office on time. The worst thing was that he liked this job – it was a great fit for someone of his cheerful disposition. He had only been with the company three months, and most of that had been spent in training. The live work was exciting and sometimes deeply fulfilling.

He put on his headphones and switched on his machine. On the far wall the performance screen was positioned so that all the operators could glance at it without standing up. Calls waiting: twelve. Average time to answer: four minutes and fifteen seconds. Average call length: eight minutes and nine seconds. Number of dropped calls today: thirteen. The screen seemed to challenge Ronnie personally. Unlucky thirteen. Half of those might have been his fault because he hadn't been at his desk to pick them up, he thought despondently.

As he answered his first call, he pinned a smile to his face and got ready to sound both cheery and sincere. "Good morning to you. My name's Ronnie. How can I help you this morning?"

*

In Ronnie's kitchen, half a mile away, a soft-scaled lizard the size of a large cat, with round sapphire eyes and long eyelashes – curious for a reptile – sat on a chair by the table, gently flicking its dark green tail. An attractive creature, as lizards go. When Ronnie's girlfriend of a year, Matilda, came into the kitchen a few minutes later, the lizard was not there.

*

Ronnie had a good day solving people's problems. Lots of positive feedback. He got home that evening feeling upbeat, but was still worried about his row with the irascible Mr Meadows. "Can we sit down and talk seriously?" he asked Matilda. "I'm scared I might lose my job," he began, avoiding eye contact. "Meadows had a real go at me today for being late. I hadn't realised it, but every day I'm seven minutes late. It's like there's a glitch in the fabric of space-time."

"A glitch, indeed!" Matilda laughed, making light of the situation, to Ronnie's relief. "Well, you must set the alarm seven minutes earlier, then," she suggested sensibly. "Then you'll be on time. It would be difficult for us if you lost your job."

"Ah, my love, always the fount of good sense. Yes, of course that's the answer. I hate waking up these days. I seem to have had such nice dreams since we've been together. Maybe you inspire my subconscious."

That night, as they went to bed, Ronnie very deliberately and specifically set the alarm on his phone for seven minutes earlier. As they kissed goodnight, he couldn't help admiring his lady's face for the thousandth time, wondering how he could have been so lucky.

*

The following morning, Ronnie leapt out of bed as soon as the alarm went off. He could hear Matilda in the kitchen preparing breakfast, sweeping the floor and singing to herself. He'd never come across anyone so clean. He remembered the tail end of a dream that had left him feeling elated. It had been something to do with beautiful landscapes and contented meditation as the sun rose. As always, the vision evaporated as soon as he tried to pin it down. He hurried through his bathroom rituals, and while getting dressed he strapped on his watch. Time was on his side; he was doing well.

But after checking a couple of messages before he came downstairs, the extra seven minutes seemed to have evaporated like his dream. It was 8.45 already. Regardless, Matilda insisted that he eat and drink something, which he did, slurping and munching with one eye on the kitchen clock. He reflected to himself that he was still in great danger of being late as he briskly walked the half-mile to the office.

Happily, Meadows was nowhere to be seen as Ronnie strode breathlessly into the ops room. He put on his headphones and pressed the computer's power button. The dashboard screen said 9.07. He was seven minutes late.

*

In Ronnie's kitchen, half a mile away, the lizard again sat on the chair by the table, gently flicking its dark green tail. It had a mug of coffee in its left claw – hand, really, as it was equipped with an opposable thumb. In its right hand it held a device the size of a breadboard with a large glowing screen, which it was studying

69

intently. Suddenly, the lizard flashed its blue eyes and flicked out its forked tongue a few times, gently touching the screen with one claw. It leaned back and put the device down on the table, breathing deeply. Evidently, it had found what it was looking for. The screen went dark. When Matilda came into the kitchen a few minutes later, the lizard was not there.

*

After work, Ronnie sat down with Matilda again and explained that, despite getting up seven minutes earlier and following his morning rituals exactly as usual, he had still arrived at work seven minutes late. Maybe he shouldn't have had breakfast; maybe there really was a glitch in the fabric of space-time? And if there was, it must be somewhere between the bedroom, the bathroom and the kitchen.

Matilda did not seem convinced. "You can't go to work without breakfast. You must have stopped to do something you don't usually do, darling. Don't worry so much."

As they settled down to sleep, Ronnie checked again that he had set the alarm for another seven minutes earlier.

*

Another morning. Another alarm. Matilda was already downstairs in the kitchen. She always got up early – well before Ronnie. In fact, he couldn't remember having seen her before breakfast in a very long time, if ever.

He rushed into the bathroom, got dressed, and walked into the kitchen, ready to head off to work. It was 8.45. That was odd. The extra time he had bought himself with the early alarm had vanished again.

"I don't understand it, my love. I don't seem to be able to get down here before quarter to nine, whatever I do. I just don't get it."

"Don't worry so much, darling. It's OK. You'll be all right. Just finish your coffee and off you go."

"I'll try not to worry, my love. Maybe I'll just set the alarm another seven minutes earlier tonight. That must fix it."

"Yes, of course, darling. Just hurry along and you'll be OK," she declared confidently, but he couldn't help but notice the look of concern in her sapphire-blue eyes.

Breathless, he opened the door to the ops room and looked at the big screen. He was seven minutes late. But no one had seen him come in...or so he thought.

Meadows made a note in his diary.

*

The lizard sat comfortably on the kitchen chair, its tail wrapped around its legs, reading *The Guardian*. It grimaced occasionally at some headline or report, blinking its eyes against the sunlight streaming in through the high window, which highlighted the sapphire glint deep within its eyelashes.

*

That night, when Ronnie came home, he related the events of the day to Matilda over spaghetti bolognese. She listened attentively as he explained whom he had managed to help, and the satisfaction of a customer saying, "Thank you so much, that's such a weight off my mind." Someone being effusively grateful and telling him he had done a good job. He loved his work, and his ratings were on the up.

As usual, Matilda had prepared dinner faultlessly, except for the large dead fly on the side of his plate. He thought he had flicked it off without her noticing, but saw her follow his movements, her tongue exploring her lips. He tucked into his bolognese without giving it another thought.

"I must set the alarm another few minutes earlier," he said, shaking his head, still worried about this bizarre problem of arriving on time.

Matilda gave him a slightly odd look. "Well, you can try," she said, without great enthusiasm, stretching her arms above her head and looking seductively over one shoulder. Ronnie walked around to her side of the table and embraced her, wondering if she was tiring of this repetitive discussion. "But if there's really a glitch in the whatever, you might be unlucky."

She was enthusiastic enough about lovemaking that night, though. So Ronnie slipped off to sleep greatly contented and dreamed profound and satisfying dreams, which as usual vanished into thin air as soon as the alarm went off. It was another seven minutes earlier. He felt ready for anything this morning, but kept one eye on the clock. Nonetheless, he was sure he had plenty of time.

As he went down to breakfast, he could smell the welcoming aromas of coffee and toast. When he opened the kitchen door there was a sudden rustling noise. Matilda was sitting at the kitchen table, clutching the breadboard.

"This was on the floor," she said, looking flustered. "How did that happen?" She strolled over to the coffee machine, filled his mug, and set it on the table as he sat down, glancing at the kitchen clock. It was almost 8.50.

"Oh, shit!" he exclaimed in disbelief. "I'm going to be late again. It's impossible. I don't believe it."

"It will be OK, darling. Everything will be OK."

Slightly peeved at her lack of concern, he returned her warm embrace but pulled away reluctantly from her fervent kisses. Must be a hangover from last night's passion. "I'm sorry, my love, but I must run – really run."

He crashed out of the door at a stiff trot. After about fifty metres, he glanced over his shoulder and saw Matilda standing on the step. Unusual, he thought. She waved, and he waved back; then he turned and ran on at an ungainly canter.

Today he was not so lucky. Meadows was in the reception area, jacket off, waving his muscular arms about and haranguing one of the receptionists. He could hardly miss Ronnie as he burst through the door, breathing heavily and uncomfortably aware that he was yet again seven minutes late.

"That's it," Meadows snarled. "We've both gone as far as we're going in this organisation. I'm the CEO and you're out. Go and clear your desk. HR will give you a dismissal letter."

Ronnie was speechless. How could he have been late again? What was happening to time when he was at home? Why could he never get onto the street before nine? He filled a cardboard box with the few personal things he kept at his desk.

Mrs La Certa, the head of personnel, came in with a white envelope for him. She reminded Ronnie of his grandma. "Never mind, dear," she said, smiling comfortingly in the manner of someone who is no longer fazed by other people's trauma. "It's a bit of a dreary job anyway, isn't it? You'll find something better. The rest of your salary will be paid at the end of the month."

Ronnie didn't have the energy to argue, but knew he would miss the customers and their positive feedback. "But I'm good at this job. I get great ratings and the customers like me – they say such nice things."

"Yes, my dear. Life can be a bit unfair sometimes. Same thing happened to my son Simon once – but it turned out to be a blessing in disguise. Never mind. I'm sure things will work out for you. Everything will be all right."

She dismissed him, but with such a sweet smile that he almost believed her for a few seconds. Then she was gone, the letter was in his hand, and gloom descended. It was disconcerting that everyone else, except the boss, seemed more confident in him than he was in himself. Ronnie looked around the room. Everyone was intent on their tasks, focused on the customers, being cheery and sincere. He picked up his box and sidled into the foyer. The receptionist was still in tears. Outside, it had begun to rain, which disguised his own tears. Utter failure. What was Matilda going to say?

Outside their front door, he juggled the cardboard box and his keys and opened the door noisily. A draught met him from somewhere. He headed for the kitchen and saw that the back door was ajar. As he put the box down on the table, he noticed a movement: something dark green disappearing through the gap in the door, like the tail of some animal.

"Matilda?" he called, knowing that he had better face the music straight away.

There was no reply.

He shrugged, distracted by a white envelope on the table which was addressed to him. Still distressed, he tore it open and read its contents, concentrating hard as its extraordinary message sank in. It was from a large insurance company, and informed him that he was being offered the customer service job he had applied and been interviewed for months before. It paid a much bigger salary than the one he'd been receiving. Could he start on Monday?

It was signed by the Director of Personnel, Matilda La Certa.

GRC, June 2022

Breakfast at the Tavern of Fury

CD AND I WERE BOTH DRIPPING WITH SWEAT. SHE LESS
so. I'd been on my feet for two days delivering training courses
in the company's conference centre just outside Tampa, Florida.
She was a lot fitter than I was. Us Aussies love to be outdoors,
and we'd decided to hit the frog and toad and walk from the

conference centre to get a bite to eat before exploring some Greek fishing village we'd heard about a way up the coast. We're just colleagues, you understand? Me and CD. Platonic friends for a long while.

As we strolled along, we'd been having a lively discussion about theories of consciousness. How I thought that consciousness could be shared under certain conditions, across both space and time; like swimming in the sea and feeling a cold current coming from somewhere. CD was a psychologist and had plenty of objections, but thought the idea had some merit. We laughed about how little we understand the basis of our feelings and experiences. Even though neuroscience has progressed so far, we still don't know how brain and mind are interrelated – if indeed they are. CD had heard some ideas about shared hallucinations when people were emotionally charged and tuned in to each other's imaginations. The local psychology was amusing too: drivers slowing down to watch two obvious nutcases walking – which no one does in Florida – and waving their arms about.

So, reaching the diner, we pushed open the door and there he was. As the cool of the AC hit us, we walked right past the bloke. He was perched on a stool by the counter, looking sullen, an empty coffee cup in front of him. He was lit up in the sunlight from the door and turned to look at us. Then he turned back, staring into the mirror behind the long wooden shelves. He didn't make a sound, even when I said g'day to him.

"Bloke's two bricks short of a barbie, I reckon," said CD quietly. "Let's get down the end outta the way."

We made our way along the wooden-floored aisle to a booth at the end, with the uncomfortable feeling of being watched.

We'd just sat down when he started sounding off. "America," he said in a loud, slow southern drawl. "What have you done to me, America?" His voice crescendoed into a howl.

Few if any of the sparse population of breakfasters looked up from their smartphones. I guessed such outbursts were not too much of a surprise to the regulars. The bloke slid from his stool and wandered up and down the aisle between the booths and the counter. He was wearing spurs. That was odd. We could hear them clinking as he moved slowly along the line of tables. The two waitresses ignored him completely. I guess he was part of the furniture – rants an' all.

"Yuh sent me to some godawful jungle to get shot at. Got malaria. Then you steal my pension, but give trillions to them damn bankers. Now yuh wanna take away my guns. Damn you, America. Damn you!"

We sat quietly, concentrating on our menus while keeping a surreptitious eye on him, hoping he would walk the other way.

Inevitably, he sat down in the booth opposite us, mumbling to himself. "America...damn...jungle...guns..."

We tried to ignore him, making small talk about the music they were playing, which drowned out some of the muttering. We studied the menus intently as the waitress approached – a pretty lady with black hair tucked up under a bonnet; her gingham uniform neatly pressed.

"What can I get y'all?" she asked.

"G'day," said CD, glancing at the opposite booth. "Full American breakfast for me, and coffee. What're you having, Bob?"

"Yeah, g'day. Me too," I added, going for the easy option. I was finding it hard to think with the mumbler in full flow. "American brekkie."

"America, America," the be-spurred bloke banged on more loudly.

"How do yuh like yuh aigs?" asked the waitress. "Sunny side up? Over easy?"

"Scrambled for me," I said. I was a bit bewildered by the local lingo.

"Sunny side up," said CD.

"Cawfee? I have espresso, cappuccino, latte, macchiato, Americano?"

"America, America." The mumbling bloke took up the refrain.

"Cappuccino," I broke in.

"Double espresso with a little milk on the side," said CD.

In our home town of Melbourne, there are about seventeen different words for coffee. I thought the list here was a bit limited, but no worries.

The waitress moved away and I watched her hips swing, the bow at the back of her apron rocking from side to side as she marched briskly down the aisle.

Just as we had been dreading, the bloke leaned across. We smelt the stale beer on his breath. "You guys not from round here, right?"

We couldn't ignore him; he was more than a bit threatening.

"Y'right, mate. We're Aussies. Just here on business."

"Ain't much business here. They took it all away. Built a damn theme park. And they think that's all we need. Make some jobs." He leaned away from us in his seat. "America...just downhill all the way." He turned to us again, waving a finger. "We used to be great, you know. Like those damn Limeys – lost their empire. We lost in Nam, Mogadishu. Now we're eaten up from the inside. They're gonna take our guns away. Can't defend ourselves against the CIA." His rant lapsed into incoherence as the waitress brought our coffees, and he was still mumbling to himself when she returned a couple of minutes later with our great American breakfasts.

"Funny how America takes over everything. Used to be called an English breakfast, this." I moved my hash browns onto a side plate, wondering why there were no baked beans. CD smiled at my remark, but was too busy eating bacon on toast to reply. "Bloody ripper, anyway!"

Then I realised that the mumbling had stopped. The bloke must have got up and walked away while the waitress was serving our breakfast with all the condiments. I hadn't heard his spurs, though.

The breakfast was really good. We tucked in like you do after an hour's walk in the hot morning sun, and called the waitress back to reorder coffee and some iced water. We were dry as a drover's dog.

"Where did that strange feller go?" I asked out of curiosity.

"What? I didn't see no one." She was smiling and looking around.

From my position in the booth I couldn't see where he'd gone. Maybe just the dunny?

The coffees appeared quickly, and we drank them in companionable silence, relieved to be free of the mumbling oddball.

"OK?" I asked CD, checking my watch. "Then we can make the fishing village before arvo."

She nodded. I often wondered why we got on so well. I think it's because we never had sex. Strangely, the subject never came up. Well, we were both married professionals. But we liked each other's company. I thought we had a great intellectual connection, anyway; maybe a shared consciousness sometimes. Let's keep it that way, I mused as I watched her walk back towards the counter. Yes, she was really attractive: long hair loose; slim legs in tight jeans. But I wasn't going to get drawn into anything that would spoil something good.

"Well, we gotta get going," I said to the waitress behind the counter as I handed over a twenty-dollar note for our breakfast. "That's OK," I added, waving away the change and leaving a tip that would be insulting in Oz, but was expected here in the land of the free. "Can you call us a cab, love?" I asked hopefully. "We're going to Tarpon Springs."

"Sure. Great place – food's *bussin* there. I'll get y'all an Uber – but you pay the driver, OK?" She was back in two minutes. "You're in luck," she said. "There's a guy going that way. Number's 2203. It says his name's Michael James. He'll be here in three. Best get outside. Y'all have a good day now."

I assured her that we all would – both of us.

*

We found a shady tree to stand under, and sure enough, in three minutes precisely, an enormous, ancient Buick with flaking bronze paint pulled in, backed up, and parked smoothly next to us under the tree.

"Y'all the folks for Tarpon Springs?"

"G'day. Yeah," I said, bending down to the window and pushing my sunnies to the top of my head. "You Mr James?"

"Michael Rhodes James here, at y'service." To say his voice was gravelly would be an understatement, but he seemed friendly enough. He even got out of the car to open the right-hand back door for CD. He was at least six foot four, solidly built, with an air of great strength, and even sported a battered cowboy hat that looked just fine on him.

I got into the left-hand back seat. The leather had seen better days and the springs were well worn, but it was comfortable enough for the thirty-mile ride.

"What is this place now?" asked Mr James.

"Just a roadside diner," I said.

"Huh," he drawled. "It used to be a baaarrr. It was called the Tavern of Fury. You hear about the troubles? Guess not. You're Limeys, ain't ya?"

"No, mate," I laughed. "We're from Oz. From Australia."

"Huh. Well, yuh speak mighty good English, I must say."

CD and I had heard that one before, and relaxed back in our seats, happy to let Mr James tell the tale he was so keen to share.

"Anyways, there was an incident a coupla years back. The Tavern of Fury was a music place, kinda. Busy at night. Band, dancing, drinking. Whatever. This guy got crazy about some shit and pulled a gun. Took a coupla girls hostage. Said he'd kill 'em because America had fucked him up. I think he was a vet. Older guy. Nam, I guess. So the cops rolled up. Did a good job. Got the customers out."

"Good work. No one hurt, then?"

"Just the guy. As the cops moved towards him, he turned the gun on himself – .44 Magnum. Not much left of his head, they say. Funny guy. Always wore spurs."

CD and I looked at each other. As the Buick pulled out onto the highway, I felt a cold shiver go down my spine and into my right leg. CD was looking pale. She slipped her arm into mine and held my hand tight.

GRC, June 2022
Based on an original incident in 2001

Jim Plays the Alphabet Game

THE DOOR TO JIM'S CAGE WAS OPEN. HE WAS WALKING on all fours across the floor of the laboratory; moving silently between the pools of cold blue light shed by the lamp-posts outside the tall sash windows. Jim had easily taught himself how to open his cage door so that he could enjoy the dark hours exploring the lab and tinkering with the equipment.

Every night he played the alphabet game. Jim thought that humans must love the alphabet. All around the laboratory there were posters and notices on the walls, all with tiny symbols which he knew meant something to humans, although he could only grasp a few of them. His language consisted of simple sounds and hand gestures. If he had had another chimpanzee to communicate with as well as the humans, he would have been a lot happier. As it was, he grew to gain some pleasure from pressing the keys with the symbols on them and trying to remember the shapes.

One machine fascinated him because he felt he could understand it better than the others. This machine had only five keys: A, C, G, T and U. He had discovered that if he pressed one button on the side of the machine a screen would light up above the keyboard, and if he pressed a key the corresponding symbol would appear on the screen. This was wonderful for Jim. It felt as if he were getting closer to understanding what it was like to be a human and to use these machines for whatever purpose they had been designed for; something he could not begin to fathom. He pressed keys at random: ACC, GTT, ACG. The symbols appeared in triplets on the screen, and he became very excited when he could predict which symbol would appear as a result of pressing a particular key.

By trial and error, he found that only four of the keys would work at any one time. He could move a switch between the keyboard and the screen to change which four. A, C and G always worked, but the switch changed whether the T or the U key would work. Jim played with the switch a few times and, this night, left it set on U. He pressed away, and soon he had a screen full of symbol triplets. He thought that it was very beautiful, and he danced around the floor for several minutes, coming back to the machine now and then to gaze at the pattern his game had created. He thumped his chest and clapped his hands. Tonight he was happier than he had been in many months.

He continued, fascinated, for more than four hours, filling screen after screen with a sequence of magic symbols. After such a mammoth exercise, he grew tired and began to yawn. He had played this game on other nights, but never for so long or with such enthusiasm. It gave him great pleasure.

It had occurred to Jim that it would not be good if the humans realised that he had been playing the alphabet game with their machines, so he always pressed the button on the side of the machine to switch off the screen afterwards. However, on this night, when he pressed the button there was a chuntering noise, but the screen stayed on. He got a bit frustrated by this and rocked the machine hard – back and forth and side to side. That made some interesting tearing noises, but still the screen stayed on. He looked at the side of the machine and could see the button in the harsh light from the street. Ah. There were two buttons: red and green. He had not seen that before. Perhaps the humans had changed something. He pressed the red one. Then he pressed the green one and the screen went dark.

Jim clapped his hands and made his way back to his cage, and once inside reached carefully through the bars and locked the door from the outside using a key that was usually left in the lock. He sometimes wondered whether the humans intended for him to escape during the night, or whether they just underestimated his ability to manipulate a simple thing like a lock and key. But these were passing images in his brain, which lacked the ability to cogitate for very long on the concept of intention.

*

Harry Hopkirk arrived at the lab at 8.30 the next morning. Jim was in his cage with the door locked. It was really a suite of cages, conforming to the now-stringent government guidelines concerning the housing of primates, with a play area, a closed-off sleeping area, and a latrine. It extended about ten metres along one wall of the lab, was three metres deep and three metres high (but for a twenty-centimetre platform on which the cage stood), and was almost the full height of the room. The play area had an earthen floor with some concrete areas, tree branches laden with swings and a tree house, ladders, a slide, some wooden seats, a water dispenser, and food bowls which were currently empty.

Harry's first jobs were to take Jim out of his cage, clean up the latrine area, which had a removable box for the animal's waste, check the water dispenser, and give Jim his breakfast. Like many young chimpanzees brought up in captivity, Jim was friendly with humans and curious about all they did, although everyone at the lab realised that as he got older he would become harder to handle and might have to be moved to more secure quarters. But right now, he would happily follow Harry around the lab as he carried out his chores, and then sit on his lap and hug him while they shared some tasty leaves and corn snacks. Harry was rather fond of Jim, and had been delighted when the management had announced that he would no longer be used as an experimental animal, but would become a kind of mascot for the lab, featuring in advertising material designed to attract corporate sponsors and customers for the genetic analysis work they carried out.

Harry's next job was to conduct some visitors around the lab, who the company hoped would become valuable sponsors. They were from a large company called Aspect Genomics, which had recently received a new and generous round of venture funding. Harry looked at his watch, and so did Jim.

"Urrrgh," said Jim.

"It's time to sit in your house," said Harry.

Immediately, Jim leapt down from Harry's lap and ran to his cage, where he sat on a wooden seat and started chewing contentedly on a bamboo stalk, which was one of a number of food and play items Harry had placed in the cage. Harry noticed that Jim was looking with interest towards the blank screen of the nucleotide sequencing machine a few metres to the right of the cage, but he couldn't see anything amiss with the machine and so thought no more of it.

Harry left the lab to greet the visitors from Aspect – six altogether – and bring them upstairs for a guided tour. There were several offices and experimental labs to show them. In one lab there were a number of long-tailed and rhesus macaque monkeys, whom Harry had helped to introduce as the main experimental subjects used in the company's research, following new international rules. Seeing so many monkeys together reminded Harry of the infinite monkey theorem: that an infinite number of monkeys typing at random would one day produce the complete works of Shakespeare. He smiled to himself at the thought. The macaques were suitable subjects for many types of study, especially regarding virus evolution and transmission. They were plentiful in the wild and the lab was careful to conform to the international guidelines on primate experimentation, thereby avoiding any critical press comment. It was no longer ethically acceptable to use anthropoid apes in potentially dangerous research. Jim did not know it, but basically, he was redundant.

"Behold, our infinite number of monkeys!" declared Harry as he led the suited-up group into the Monkey Lab. It was vital that no organic material found its way from the humans to the macaques or vice versa.

Several of the group chuckled at his remark, recognising the reference. The group asked Harry a few questions about the macaques and the experimental regimes and then signalled that they would like to move on. Once they had de-suited and scrubbed their hands, Harry led them down the corridor and unlocked and opened the door of Jim's Lab, as it had begun to be called. He ushered the group inside. They were greeted by Jim chattering away at the door of his cage. Jim was a little disappointed that he was not immediately let out to play with them; he loved receiving visitors. Harry signalled to him to be quiet. Jim put his forefinger to his lips conspiratorially, and Harry began his long explanatory speech.

"Welcome to our nucleotide sequencing laboratory, where we unravel the encoding of life." He was rather pleased with that phrase. "It's here that we can both sequence the genomes of DNA- and RNA-based organisms, and furthermore synthesise genome sequences which can be used for therapeutic purposes. This has only become possible over the past few years, and what we learned from the Covid pandemic has been vital in creating a basic model for the preparation of gene sequences." Moving into marketing mode, Harry described the booming field of synthetic biology and its benefits which could revolutionise medicine, cure intractable diseases, and extend lifetimes. "In our view, our nucleotide sequencing and synthesis machine is the state of the art in genomics."

The group admired the machine from afar and did not seem to want to get too close to it.

"Isn't there some danger in synthesising genomes?" asked one of the visitors; an American lady with long hair and glasses, who did not look as if she would be easy to convince otherwise.

"Well, to be frank, yes, there are dangers," explained Harry. "But we conduct sequencing and synthesis experiments under tightly controlled laboratory conditions. We can insert new sets of genes into microbes and use them to generate proteins which have beneficial properties. Of course, it's theoretically possible that a rogue state could use the technology to cause harm, but that's more a political problem than a scientific one."

"I see," said the lady. "And here you have a machine that can be used for synthesising RNA a few yards from a cage containing a primate."

Jim looked up when he heard the word 'primate', recognising it as a probable reference to him. He chattered a bit but then kept his head down, hoping that Harry would let him out to play with these visitors.

"Well, yes, but the microbial preparation devices behind the nucleotide machine are confined in a separate clean area on the other side of the wall, and maintained at negative pressure so that no material can escape."

The lady looked at him coldly, but let the question drop.

"If I may explain further?" Harry continued. "DNA and RNA, as you'll be aware, are the instructions for life and are the same across all life forms on this planet, and if you include viruses, they're the same across non-living replicators as well. Each of the twenty amino acids that make up a protein is coded by sixty-one triplet codons."

"So," one of the visitors asked, "if there are sixty-one codons and only twenty amino acids, does that mean that each amino acid may be defined by more than one codon?"

"Exactly – with a couple of exceptions. Nothing is simple in nature," replied Harry with a smile, delighted that the group were on the ball. There was a nodding of heads. "In fact, each species has specific codon preferences for the coding of each amino acid, which is called codon bias." He continued, explaining that each of the three letters of a codon corresponds to one or other of the bases adenine (A), cytosine (C), guanine (G) and thymine (T), and that in RNA, uracil (U) replaces thymine. He made a particular point of setting out in some detail the precautions the lab had put in place for handling dangerous material and to prevent any pathogen ever escaping. That could be, he said, potentially disastrous. "So we have designed the whole process with safety as our primary concern."

Despite the highly technical content of Harry's presentation, all eyes were focused on him with apparent good comprehension. This was not a group of people who could be blinded by science, but Harry preferred this kind of audience. There could be lively discussion and new ideas might emerge.

"How long would it take to synthesise, say, a 30,000-base RNA sequence, like a virus?" asked the American woman.

"Well, in terms of creating the instructions, just a few hours once you had the sequence set out. You would feed the sequence into the nucleotide synthesiser using a file upload, but then you would make modifications using the keyboard to adjust the sequence. You could actually input the whole thing by hand, but the possibility of error doing it that way would be large, and the RNA would probably not be viable. After that, the machine would take the sequence, synthesise the actual RNA, and insert it into a microbe, where we would expect it to begin replicating – as long as the microbe was suitable. We can engineer the microbes as well."

"Indeed, as I thought, a quick process. This is very interesting to us. But I don't think you should have an ape in the same lab space, no matter how good your airflow control is. In fact, I'm surprised you're still using chimpanzees."

"We're not using him for experiments. He was used for a while three or four years ago when he was very small, and he survived a couple of nasty infections with engineered microbes. That led to some useful therapeutic discoveries. But like everyone else, we've since discontinued the experimental use of anthropoid apes. Now we have the full sequence of the macaques' DNA, we can work more readily with them. Jim is now a lab mascot, really."

"Jim?"

"Yes – sorry, this is a bit infantile, but he's referred to as Jim-Panzee."

The group burst into laughter, but the American lady did not smile.

*

A couple of days later, the general manager called Harry into his office.

"You did a great job with the Aspect Genomics people."

"Thanks," said Harry, smiling in pleasure at the compliment. "I did my best. They seemed enthusiastic about the synthesis machine."

"Yes – they're going to commission us to prepare some RNA for therapeutic use. They're supporting cancer programmes that are working on that approach."

Harry nodded; he was familiar with the work.

"They have one stipulation, though," continued the GM, looking away for a moment. "We have to euthanise Jim."

"What?!" spluttered Harry, in shock at such an outrageous demand from outsiders. "Why? What's their problem with Jim? Do they think there's something wrong with him?"

"That's exactly their concern. We don't know what's wrong with Jim, if anything. But an ape who has potentially been exposed to any pathogens coming through our synthesis process could, as the Aspect people say, become very dangerous."

"But he's only in that room because we had nowhere else to keep him after we stopped using him for the experimental programmes."

"Yes, I fully understand that, Harry, and I know you're fond of him."

"He's…he's almost like a child to me." Harry was horrified at the turn in the conversation, and at the same time he was surprised by how strong his feelings were.

"But you know," continued the GM, avoiding looking Harry full in the face, "that in a few years he'll become unmanageable. He could tear your arm off if he got angry. He would have to go to a zoo then, and no zoo would accept him with his background of potentially dangerous experimentation."

Harry was silent for a moment, trying to think of an alternative.

"I suggest we get this over with as soon as possible," said the GM, standing to make it clear that the discussion was at an end. "We can do the job in the morning."

"Let me think about it," said Harry, his voice wavering.

"I don't think we have a choice. You know that animal is living on borrowed time already. And anyway, with the new investment we need the space for more equipment."

Harry grimaced at that. How could anyone sweep aside the existence of a living creature just to make space for equipment? He stood up, muttered an "OK" to the GM, and left the room.

Outside, he began to weep. He walked to the lab, turned down the lights, let Jim out of his cage and hugged him, rocking him like a baby. Jim could see Harry's tears, and tried to wipe them away gently with his hand. That only brought forth more tears, so Harry let Jim run around for a while, enjoying himself, and then he leapt back into Harry's arms and was gently rocked off to sleep. Harry held him for maybe an hour before he could bring himself to lead the chimpanzee by the hand to his cage, and lock him in for the last time.

*

When Harry unlocked the lab in the morning and came in to take Jim on his last walk, he had tears in his eyes again. Jim wouldn't understand; he would just give Harry his love and trust. But there was none of the usual chirruping as Harry approached the cage. Jim lay on the floor, his breathing shallow; his eyes puffy and bloodshot. Harry was horrified. He rushed from the room and within five minutes returned with a colleague, Zoe, an experienced microbiologist. They both looked at Jim's small frame that lay twitching on the floor of the cage.

"What on earth can be wrong?" asked Harry, feeling deep concern for his primate friend who only the previous evening had been cheerful and full of life.

"If I were to hazard a guess," said Zoe, listening carefully to the pattern of Jim's breathing, "it looks like a serious, fast-acting virus. Look at those sores on his face. I think we should suit up. You never know how likely a spillover is from chimps to humans. That's how HIV started, after all, and maybe Ebola."

They left the room and locked the door. Both took showers and put on biological isolation garments. Then they approached the lab again. Zoe nodded as Harry produced the key. As the door opened, there was an eerie silence.

Jim lay dead on the floor – outside of the cage, between the open door and the nucleotide machine. His arm was outstretched towards the machine. To their horror, in the sunlight streaming in from the tall windows, Harry and Zoe could see that the machine had been wrenched a few millimetres away from the wall, creating a tear in the thick plastic sealing, and the microbial clean room behind was open to the air.

GRC, February 2023

It Can't Be Christmas Again Already?

DEAR DARLINGS!

What a year it's been!!! And Christmas is here again, so I'd like to catch you up on the family news. And I have to say – sorry, but I'm a bit down at the moment, if you really want to know!

That nice Mr Johnson – isn't he a sweetie? Just like a little boy, and he likes *Peppa Pig* and the Oompa Loompas so much, he can't be *all* bad, I thought. But then we were sitting there in our nice house in Ibiza and people were saying we had to leave the common market Europe thing and we'd all have to go, because of some deal nice Mr Johnson had done with the Germans. I was gobsmacked. I mean, we'd been living very comfortably in Ibiza with no paperwork since Dave got banged up in Malta a few years back. Oh, sorry, I forgot to say – Dave was let out this year, in February. No time off for good behaviour – just like I thought! Anyhow, more about him later. He's such a naughty boy!!

But this Brexit thing… Anyway, it was the 1 April when that nice policeman Pedro dropped in. He's been a friend for simply ages! He said that technically we were all illegal immigrants as we hadn't filled in a form to become nationalised or something. I said that was strange 'cause we've spent plenty of money and I thought that it was good for the economy – certainly good for the bars! But he said, because of some questionnaire they did years ago in the UK – one we couldn't fill in because we'd lived abroad for a while by then – we were now going to be thrown out of our home! So maybe Mr Johnson isn't so nice after all? Isn't our government supposed to protect its citizens, not get them thrown out of their homes – which we own legit, of course, mainly? I don't get it.

So Graham had to leave his nice job in the bar down the road, and Cheryl said she's going to marry her Spanish boyfriend so she can be nationalised. Of course, that set Dave off on one of his rants. Funny – I almost missed those while he was away!

"She ain't marryin' no foreigner," he said, going extremely red in the face and waving his arms about. "That's why we left England: because there wuz too many foreigners there."

I didn't quite get the logic of that, to be honest, but I kept quiet. Always the best thing to do while Dave's on a rant.

Anyway, so Pedro the policeman says, in the nicest possible way, we have to go back to where we came from. Where've I heard that before? But then he sits down, taking his policeman's hat off, and says how sorry he is about all of this. It's just stupid politicians trying to hang on to their jobs. How can we be bad people today, when yesterday we were good people, contributing to the local economy? Even Dave. I had to agree with him.

Really, I don't get this elections thing. These political parties say they want us to vote for them and they promise all sorts of goodies, but then they don't do much of anything, and what they do, they stuff up. People said that the lady who was the boss after nice Mr Johnson would make England the Switzerland of Europe. But haven't we got a Switzerland already? Why do we only get to choose between people who talk, talk, talk? Why can't we choose between real experts who actually know what the hell they're doing? Never mind me; I'm sure I don't understand it. It's better now we're part of India, though – at least the curries will be good. In Spain we could just avoid all that and sit quiet, giving the family a chance to grow up somewhere nice and warm and get a good job they like.

So now we're back in England. Back in Ilford, even. Bit of a shock, coming back. The old semi was OK, though, and the tenants were very nice about moving out quickly, especially when Dave had one of his rants at them on the phone. I think they decided not meeting him in person was the best thing.

And we had to come back to the virus too. Of course, we'd all had our vaccinations by then, so we're healthy enough, but I'm afraid Mum succumbed at the end of 2020, just before the New Year. I couldn't go to the funeral because of the restrictions.

Despite what the politicians were up to. Not even Dad could. But one of the police officers who used to chase her motorbike down Death Hill wrote me a nice little letter. He said how sad he and his mates were to see her go that way. She would have preferred a massive pile-up on the M20, or a knife fight with a chapter of Hells Angels on Wrotham Hill, he said. They were just a bit ashamed that the only way they'd ever been able to catch up with her was by going to her funeral. They were only allowed to go because they got permission to form a guard of honour. I was touched by that. We're keeping her bike in the living room. Dad polishes it every day.

Dad's OK, though. He married his nurse, Gladys, in the summer and they now live in the annex down the garden. Not a big surprise, really! But he still loves Mum. You can see from the way he polishes that bike, as if he was giving Mum a nice cuddle. He was heartbroken not to get to the funeral. Sometimes Gladys helps him, and I see tears in her eyes. From time to time I wonder what the three of them used to get up to. But it's no one's business but theirs, is it?

Of course, I had to tell my friend Jim that Dave was coming out, so that was a bit of a downer too. Jim had been so helpful, sorting out the cash from the Bulgarian property deals, the paperwork for the Spanish electrics, and one or two other things. That's how we've kept going all this time. Pity he didn't know about the nationalisation. He'd heard something about it, he said, but he explained that David Frost only got it sorted out at the last moment. "David Frost?!" I said. I used to love him when he was on telly all those years ago doing "That was the week that was" – very witty man. And he looks quite sprightly even now, on the news. Although, he must be over eighty. Can't imagine why they gave him the job at his age. Jim said it was too late to do anything about the residential nationalisation thing once the rules were agreed. Actually, I think he wanted to get out of the picture before Dave reappeared. You can't blame him really, seeing as how Dave had just done five years for manslaughter – bless him!

So, we did try to do the nationalisation papers. Pedro the police officer was kind enough to get the forms and he explained what they needed to know. But there was a problem, what with Dave's criminal record and the source of our income not being exactly straightforward.

Anyway, that's it. We're back in Ilford!! It never seems to stop raining, it's three degrees (I only speak centigrade these days), and we have a shiny red motorbike in the living room instead of Mum. But you can't complain, can you? The rest of us have survived. Dave's got a steady job driving a van in London for some Maltese blokes he met in jail in Valetta. Seems reliable work, but mainly in the evenings, and he does come home looking a bit shaky sometimes and needs a nip or two of whisky before slumping down in front of the telly. He seems to be much more interested in the news now than he used to be. He says he brushed up on various dimensions of his education while in jail. Well, he certainly didn't use words like 'dimensions' before, so the clink must have done him some good. And he did take me for a lovely anniversary dinner at the Savoy in London a few weeks ago. Van driving must be better paid these days!

What about Graham and Cheryl, you're bound to ask? I'm glad to tell you that Cheryl did marry her Spaniard, Carlos. Dave's rant seemed to wear off when he realised that Carlos's father was among the top thirty billionaires in Europe. She's got a nice house overlooking the sea on the Spanish Riviera with, I think, fourteen bedrooms. Or is it sixteen? Anyway, enough for a family visit.

And Graham? He's fallen on his feet too, in a funny way. I think I said he'd been practising his guitar since he lost his job and got a bit bored with the fishing. He was asked to play in a bar, and the Spanish owner managed to get him a work permit so he could stay in Spain. I think Pedro helped a bit with that, after I offered him some savoury prawns – one of my specialities! Then some bloke from the local radio broadcast a *gig* – I think they call it – at the bar. Actually, it's quite a big bar. There were about 500 people there. And now our Graham's a bit of a star and doing *gigs* in Germany and Holland as well as all round Spain and Portugal.

It's an ill wind, as they say. But me – I have to get used to being with Dave again, with his rants and his sulks, but at least he's kind to me most of the time, and much more generous than he used to be. I miss Graham and Cheryl. They were always good company while I was waiting for Dave to come out, and when Jim wasn't around. I hear from them, of course. We talk on the Zoom thingy – we've all learned to do that, haven't we??! But it's not the same. I miss Mum too. Sometimes I chat to her motorbike and I'm glad it's still in one piece.

All I ever wanted from life, really, was to be happy, despite it all…and not to have to worry about money and paperwork. So maybe what you lose, you just have to leave behind and look on the bright side! Keep calm and think of England, don't they say? Or is that something else? For me, I think of that house in Ibiza where we had such happy times. No more.

Anyway, all my love to you all, darlings!!

Samantha (and Dave – although he's out somewhere at the moment, driving the van. He told me not to wait up.)

xxxx

GRC, February 2023

The Universal Trade Naming Enforcement Agency

The ticker is running across the bottom of the news broadcast screen:

> *Dateline March 3, 2037: Security team find two gold buttons and a Rolex on Oval Office floor. No sign of the President.*

That's the news today, but it was a long time ago when this story started. I first heard the rumour just before Christmas 2020 – on NBC. They reported that this Israeli scientist had claimed that the President had met a group of aliens and made a deal which would stop any trouble between them and us earthlings. Now, that sounded pretty far-fetched at the time, so, y'know, I thought I'd look into it. I mean, were there any records of this meeting? They keep records, don't they, presidents? They have records of everything. They sit in the Oval Office, they have meetings, they record them, then they have minutes that are written down and those go into the archive, don't they? It's public property, national security and such. So where in the archives were these meeting notes? I thought I would ask someone.

I was a blogger – 'journalist' they called us in the old days, but now there are no journals any more so the title makes no sense. Still, I would prefer to be called a journalist than a blogger – sounds more like a real job. So that was what I did to earn a crust. I asked people questions and then I wrote up something that some clown would buy. And sometimes, well, it would go wild on the airwaves and I might get sued, and my lawyer would see them off. I had a reputation to keep up, after all.

Anyway, y'know, as a result of my rather complicated life I had a lot of contacts around the Hill, so I asked about. I found someone who had been on the White House staff at that time who should be able to tell me whether there was a record of this meeting with the aliens, right? But they couldn't find anything, could they? No surprise there. So then I wondered, was this all just fake news? Some fantasy or other? Or was there some other explanation?

Now, this Israeli guy; this scientist, he was about eighty-seven, so I was told. So there could have been an explanation.

You know, it could have been that he had gone a bit senile or something, so maybe he was making the whole thing up? Maybe he didn't even know he was making it up? He probably believed it, but he was making it up nonetheless – amazing what the brain does to rationalise things. And this President guy – well, he's no longer in the White House. Replaced twice over.

I had no intention of going up and asking him what he thought, 'cause the chances were he would make something up to make himself look good. He was a politician, after all. That's what they do, even now. On the other hand, the Israeli scientist, well, he might have been having a joke to get the media worked up a bit with some cranky idea. So, back in 2020 he said, the President met these aliens and did some deal with them, didn't he? So that's the second possible explanation.

But I wondered about this. Like, it was a pretty wild claim, and obviously the media had heaps of fun with it for a few days. They ridiculed the Israeli scientist, but uncharacteristically the old President kept quiet on the topic – strange, I thought. But then I went back to my friend who'd been on the White House staff and I said, "I know you told me there's no record of this meeting, but do you know anyone who might know anything about it?"

The guy wasn't keen to help, but he owed me for something that had happened back in Bangkok in 1991. He was still a bit nervous that somebody was gonna blab, so he said, "OK, I'll give you a hand."

And, behold – a few days later, he called me. "Look, I've found this guy, he's told me something about this meeting. In fact, he was there! And I got him recorded on the cell phone. Do you wanna hear it? You're not gonna like it."

"You know me," I said. "I like anything that will make me a few bucks."

So I arranged to meet him. In the parking lot of a government building in DC – where else? He handed over the cell phone (it was a burner), and I made a couple of promises about Bangkok – whoa, whoa, what a night! Then I went back to my office and sat down with my feet on the desk like my hero Philip Marlowe, with a cup of coffee and a vape, and I started listening. And this – I'm tellin' you now – is exactly how it went, after a bit of introductory interrogation from my friend, who had his own markers to call in.

The story began. My friend first: "Well, you know that old Israeli scientist who said that the President had a meeting with aliens and agreed something with them about…what do they call it? The Galactic Federation? Now, of course there wasn't a record of the meeting, but that President was a bit sloppy on records, as we all knew, right? I want you to tell me in your own words exactly what happened that morning, without any interruptions from me."

So the guy from the Oval Office begins: "Well, it wasn't quite like you might think. For a start, this alien the President met was about two foot tall and he looked like a person – only with green skin and hair. He just appears in front of the desk, which the President's leaning on, talking to me about some shit. One moment he isn't there, the next he is. He rattles away in an incomprehensible language for a while, and he's fiddling about with a…uh…kinda machine he's holding. Suddenly, there's plain English coming out of it. He's saying that earth people have broken the Intergalactic Law, and the President has to fix it to avoid some dreadful punishment.

"'Wow, wow, wow. So what kind of law are we breaking, according to you?' the President asks, standing up to his full height and staring down at the little green man two or three yards away.

"'Trade naming copyright,' says the alien firmly. Then he puts his speaking device on a tripod that he seems to conjure out of thin air and folds his arms.

"'What kinda crap is that?' says the President – a touch insensitively, I thought. He's getting red in the face by this time. 'Well, what is it exactly that we've done wrong? According to you – wherever you're from.'

"The alien's waving his little green arms about, trying to explain. 'It's the way you people go around using the word "universal".'

"'Universal?' says the President, and raises one eyebrow as if he's thinking that this is some kind of con using a clever robot.

"'Yeah,' says the alien, rapidly picking up the vernacular. 'Universal. You sure as hell know that "universal" is an adjective that means "the whole of the universe", and yet you here on earth go around calling things "Universal Studios", "Universal Music", "Universal Television", "Universal Soap", universal toilets and things like that, and we're incensed about that, because these companies are not universal at all. They're only on earth, and maybe only in one place on earth. And the royalties that are due…just humongous – you wouldn't even want to think about the amount.'

"So the alien, he's really going off on this, he says, 'Look, you've got your Interface Netbook FlixTube thing, and you only gotta look on that. There are thousands of people on your planet using the word "universal" in a totally inappropriate fashion. I'm sure I don't need to remind you that it's an abuse of intellectual property rules that *are* universal. All sentient creatures know that. In fact, several inhabitants of your planet are fully aware of this abuse, and they reported it to us. The dung beetles are not happy, and nor are certain species of intelligent grass and several kinds of lizards.'

"So the President is getting a bit pissed with this. Here's this two-foot-tall guy telling him that the whole of humanity on planet earth is enraging all the aliens because of companies using the word 'universal' in naming things – and upsetting the dung beetles and the lizards. He says, 'What are you blaming me for? I'm only the President of the great and mighty US of A, not the whole world, am I?'

"'Now, you got a point there,' says the alien, scratching his little green ear and calming down a bit. 'But come on: we've been looking at your newspapers and your broadcast media and your Internet Faceflix Netbook WhatTube things for ages, and we can see that this country here – the United Whatever-It-Is – is lording it over most of the planet and causing a lot of trouble in the meantime. So we figure we should hold you responsible for the infractions.'

"'No, no,' says the President, getting red in the face again, infuriated that he could be held to account for stuff everyone else on the planet has done too, 'that's not how it works at all. We're a kinda free society, you know. People can call themselves what they like, subject to various trade naming practices that we have, uh, a bureau to look after.'

"That sounds weak even to me, and the alien jumps in like lightning. 'Your *bureau* is not doing a particularly good job, then, is it? They're letting people call themselves "Universal This" and "Universal That", and they're not universal at all, are they? A lot of them are just round-the-corner shops. I mean, something like Universal Mart that only exists in Soda Springs, Idaho, is clearly trampling all over the crucial trade naming conventions that my

105

agency is out there to uphold. You gotta comply or there'll be the mother of all lawsuits – and worse.'

"'Well,' says the President, who's never been much worried about lawsuits, 'you can't blame me for that, can you? We got freedom – we let people go around calling themselves what they like. We got celebrities call themselves "Ice Dog" or "Big Daddy Smoothie" or "Ol' Man G". I mean, we got *some* rules, but we ain't got no rule that says you can't call yourself "Universal This" or "Universal That". Stands to reason – we're not hurting anyone, are we?'

"'Oh yes, you damn well are,' says the alien through his translating device, and I'm amazed that he gets just the right inflection on the swear word. 'There are billions in unpaid taxes that should be going toward the upkeep of the cosmic galaxies. There are zimphainfs out there starving to death because you are permitting unlicensed nomenclature. And don't ask me to describe the ecology of zimphainfs.'

"'Don't you get uppity with me, young...whatever you are. I could have you thrown out right now,' says the President, reaching over the desk for the telephone.

"'I don't think it would be a good idea to try that,' says the alien, stepping forward a few small paces. 'I'm surrounded by a force field, you know. If you or your goons touch me, your hands will be blown to bits.' It's hard to make a menacing look seem convincing when you're two foot tall, but the alien pulls it off, and continues in the same aggressive vein. 'Are you ignorant? I'm a representative of the Universal Trade Naming Enforcement Agency, so I can materialise wherever I like. I come from head office and you should respect what I have to say.'

"At this, the President laughs out loud. 'What?' he says, wagging his finger threateningly and foaming at the mouth as if he's about to burst. 'You are a two-foot-high alien who looks like a little guy with green hair. And you're trying to scare *me*?! You don't want to threaten me, punk.'

"The alien bristles dangerously, his green hair glowing violet at the tips. 'If you're trying to make me mad, you're doing a very good job. I'm here to warn you and the people of this planet that you are in danger of being severely punished because you have transgressed the code of the Universal Trade Naming Enforcement Agency.'

"'Ah!' says the President, raising his capacious eyebrows as if spotting a chink in the alien's armour. 'So you call yourselves "universal" but you won't let us do it?'

"'Well, that's because we *are* universal, aren't we, you moron? We police the entire universe in terms of trade naming practices.' The alien's voice fills the room as if from a thousand-watt speaker.

"As the echo dies away, it's as if a light suddenly switches on in the President's head and his expression changes from one of fiery debate to grave concern. His face tells the story: at last he grasps that this is not some kind of practical joke. If he hadn't been suffering from an overdose of narcissism, he would have realised earlier that something two foot tall suddenly appearing in his secure office did indeed indicate the use of some kind of unusual power. His jaw drops, and I can almost hear the cold shiver running down his spine. He takes a step back and looks at me for support. Here we are, arguing with someone who can materialise anywhere, protected by a force field, and press the claims of a powerful agency that can do irreparable harm to the President's prospects of re-election and my future employment. Oh, and to the planet too, of course.

"The President moves away from the alien, rounds the desk, sits down heavily, scratches his head and adjusts his hairpiece. He speaks more tentatively than I've ever heard him speak before. 'Are you seriously expecting me to believe that you can go all over the universe and police universal trade naming practices?'

"'You can believe what you like, but I tell you, you'll have another think coming when we come along and punish you personally for illegal trade naming practices on your planet,' the alien responds firmly. 'You've no idea what we could do to you. We don't play games. Not at the Universal Trade Naming Enforcement Agency.'

"The President looks down at his hands spread out on the empty desk and lets out a massive sigh. He's clearly disturbed by this conversation, but manages to articulate a clever question. 'So are you going to give us some time to sort this out?' he says, in a more conciliatory tone.

"'Yes, of course: we can give you the statutory restitution period.'

"'Eh?' says the President eloquently.

"'You've got no idea of the rules, have you?' Exasperated, the alien puffs himself up and opens a digital pad to read from. 'Article sixty-three of the Universal Trade Naming Enforcement Code of Conduct is perfectly clear. Paragraph five, sub-paragraph iii (a): "An offender has sixteen years to eliminate the abuses throughout their planetary domain."' He reads the rule out sternly, adding, 'I quoted the time period in your earth years, for your convenience.'

"'Sixteen years,' mutters the President. 'So you'll come back in sixteen years? Is it exactly sixteen years, or could it be, you know...' He clears his throat and scratches his head before asking, 'Might it be thirteen years? Or twenty-one years?' To my mind, he seems to be calculating something.

"'No,' says the alien. 'We organise it, so it'll be sixteen years and about three months on your planet when I and my colleague next materialise in this office. You better have it fixed by then or you're in big trouble – personally. Our motto is "Hold the bastards responsible". It's the leaders who are accountable – we don't persecute the poor offenders when it's the leaders who make the blunders.'

"At this point the President frowns, but then he looks across the room at me with a slight smile. He politely asks for a time out and moves toward me. I'm feeling shaky, and I reckon I'm looking pale. I notice the alien glance at a device attached to his wrist and shake his head.

"The President whispers to me, 'Get me that Israeli guy on the phone – you know, the science geek who was here yesterday. He should still be at the Hilton on K Street.'

"I get the guy on the cell phone and hand it over to the President. He speaks for five minutes and closes the phone looking a little less ill at ease.

"He puts his arm round my shoulder and turns me round so we're both facing the wall. He mutters under his breath to me, 'Sixteen years, Greeny said, right? Well, it's pretty unlikely I'm gonna be around in sixteen years' time, so maybe I can just ignore this and it'll go away. Maybe the whole planet will go away in sixteen years, but I'll be gone before that anyway, so it won't bother me, will it?'

"'No, Mr President,' I say, my voice a little shaky, as the President releases my shoulder from his grip and we turn round.

"The alien has vanished."

*

So here we are in Washington DC in 2037 and there has just been this extraordinary news item on the DataTube: 'US President missing. Only gold buttons and a Rolex found in the Oval Office.' Even at my age, the old journalistic instincts roar back. Maybe I could get the Pulitzer after all? I never managed to publish anything much from the audio recording – apart from my promises to my White House contact, it was just too far out there. The only ones interested were the 'A hamster ate my gran' mags, which I didn't want to sully my reputation with.

So I call my old White House guy. He's nearly eighty now, but he may still be susceptible to graymail.

"Oh, I was kinda expecting a call from you," he said nervously.

"Any ideas?" I asked. I like open questions.

"Well, y'know, that old President deliberately never left a memo about that encounter, thinking he wouldn't have to face the enforcement guys again personally. Although he did make an unscheduled stop in Soda Springs, Idaho, at one point. Anyway, he was right: he's not around now, as you know. So, the new guy? Well, he's only been in the job a few weeks and he'd have known nothing. I can only guess at what happened. But it seems like it didn't go well."

*

President Xavier Abdulkadir looked up from his desk in the Oval Office. It was a Tuesday. He had just finished a tense call with the Chinese Premier about noodle exports from the Spratly Islands, which he had conducted alone. His aides had listened in from their own desks, and were now making copious notes. Then, to his surprise, two medium-height men in black suits, who looked like twins, were standing between his big desk and the doorway. They were neatly dressed, and each carried a black briefcase with the initials 'UTNEA' on it in Roman script.

"You must be expecting us," intoned the first man in a monklike fashion. He looked very serious indeed. The President hadn't even had the opportunity to get a word out. "We're from the Universal Trade Naming Enforcement Agency, as you are no doubt aware. It is sixteen years and three months since we visited your predecessor's predecessor, who we understand has gone to his grave without completing his sacred cleansing task."

"Eh?" replied the President eloquently. Normally a jovial individual, well used to practical jokes, he nevertheless reached for the panic button under his desk, but the spokesman strode toward him, holding out his hand. The President stood and shook it across the desk. It was clammy.

"We note some progress," said the spokesman. "But it is insufficient to assuage our wrath."

"Eh?" replied the President again. "What wrath?! What the hell do you mean, coming in here unannounced, talking about wrath? Is this some kinda joke? I'll get security right now." But strangely, he found himself unable to bend, and he could not reach the panic button. Now he was really scared, expecting guns to be produced from the men's neat suits at any moment.

"But we are fair and just at the Agency. We can see that your predecessor – twice removed – used his influence to close down some companies and cause others to change their names. He made a personal visit to Soda Springs, Idaho. I don't know if you are aware."

"Soda Springs, Idaho? What the f*** are you talking about?!"

"Your predecessor must have left you the documentation, surely? I must confess that last time it was unwise of me to materialise as a rather obvious visitor from a different world, but this time we are better prepared."

"Get out, right now!" shouted the President, trying to step forward. He found himself unable to move. This was terrifying.

Help! Help me! he tried to scream at the top of his voice; yet no words emerged.

"Let me explain," said the alien, with the ghost of a smile, but advancing apace toward the big desk. "I really don't know why you people have such poor communication, but this is the situation." He went through the same spiel as he had sixteen years previously, but with less arm-waving. "So," he continued, arms extended in a gesture of conciliation, "progress has been made, but we need you to commit right now to completing the elimination of the word 'universal' from all trade names on this planet. If you promise – and we understand the sacredness of the institution of promising on this planet – then we will allow you to continue in office."

Suddenly, the President found himself able to sit down. "OK, OK, whatever you say," he squeaked, and surreptitiously pushed the panic button.

"Thank you. Now, when your security people burst in, we would like for you to shake our hands and say again, 'Yes, we undertake to do whatever you say.' And then we will be on our way, but we will return within three years, at which point you will still be in office, so you had better ensure the elimination of infringing epithets by then."

The door burst open and three marines in full combat uniform stood momentarily frozen to the threshold.

"It's OK, guys," said the President in as normal a voice as possible. "These gentlemen were just leaving. So," he turned back to the besuited aliens, "we will do what you ask."

As he uttered the last word, the marines found themselves able to move forward, and regardless of the President's words, they held their weapons at the ready.

"That is wise of you." The alien spokesman hadn't turned his gaze from the President, despite the sound of the marines thundering into the room. His voice contained no hint of a threat. He seemed almost graciously thankful, as if he had been promised a donation for a butterfly sanctuary.

The President shook the aliens' hands, which were still clammy. Then they turned toward the door and the marines moved aside to let them past.

"Cosmic, guys," said the President.

The two aliens stopped and turned to stare at him. You have never seen such contempt in the eyes of a human.

The words "Oh shi—" still hung in the air as the President's bulky frame evaporated. Two gold buttons from his jacket and the gold Rolex from his wrist hit the carpet and bounced – only once.

GRC, November 2022

Generation Gap

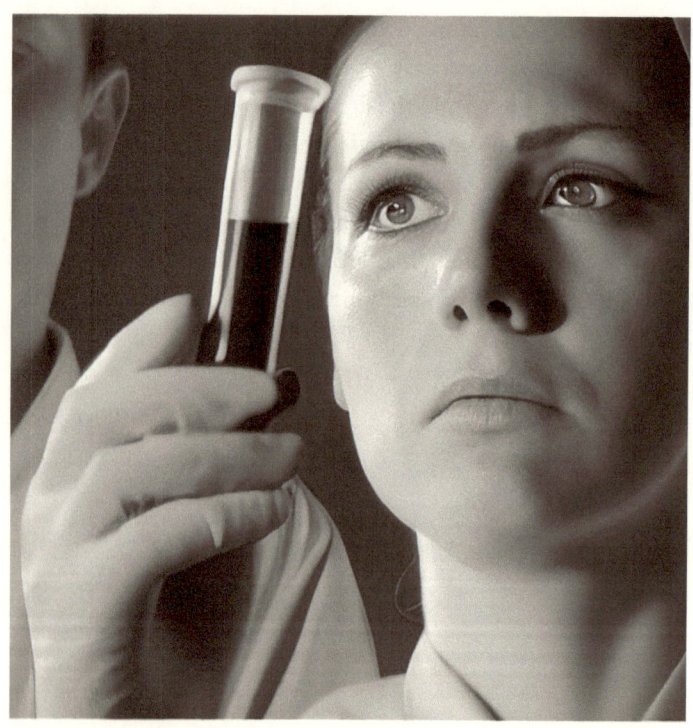

My dear grandson,

I'm not quite sure how to address you but I think 'grandson' is good. After all, I'm not your father, so I should have another name for you to use. One that's fitting. If you're happy with using a title for me, then 'grandad' would be nice.

If you're reading this on your eighteenth birthday as I requested, I think you're ready to understand what I have to tell you. And, if my wishes have been followed, you will know that there is something remarkable about you. I will come to that.

Along with this letter, you'll also have come into possession today of a strange artefact. I hope it has stood the test of time. If my surmises about scientific progress were correct, it may now be nearly a hundred years old. It may look a bit like a piece of old wood, but it is in fact a tooth embedded in plastic resin. To be more precise, it's a tooth of mine. Perhaps you'll find that rather macabre, but please don't let it disturb you. It's a memento of considerable significance for us both, and I hope you're willing to look after it. This letter, too, I hope you will find helpful and worth preserving as a personal gift from me to you.

Your world will be very different from mine, for you were born well over a hundred years later than me. When this letter reaches you, I will have been dead forty or fifty years. I've never met the fine lady who carried you from conception to birth and who has taken care of you for all of your life so far. She wasn't born when my body chemistry ceased functioning after what was in my time a long life. By the late 2020s, we were confident that life expectancy and quality of life would by your day have improved to such an extent that yours would be a wonderful generation to be born into. Now you can expect to live to 150 years or more, barring accidents. We were lucky to get to eighty, and by then few of us could do much, except make plans for what could never be.

In my world, few people understood history. I came to the view that understanding history is the one key we have to both our past and your future. We're formed by history, but we are not bound by it. I was a scientist, but I knew that history could give me a perspective on my work that would make me a better scientist. What does 'better' mean? I think seeing the context of my discoveries has helped me to grasp the flow of universal consciousness that I inhabited, so I knew where to go next. It gave me a choice. I am going to give you a bit of history, and I hope it will grip your imagination so much that you'll want to learn from my humble thoughts. I want to share a way of thinking – living – that I know will make sense for you. In my experience, eighteen-year-old boys quite like to listen to their grandads' stories, while their fathers can seem a bit forbidding. I imagine you have a father to rely on – the husband of your mother – but sometimes a stepfather has other agendas, so maybe you'll like my stories. In a letter like this I'll try not to be too long-winded, though. I just want to give you a perspective on life that you can get no other way. And may I give you some advice? I hope you won't mind – I'm not trying to make myself out to be wiser than I am, but if someone had told me a few things when I was eighteen, I would've made fewer mistakes and fewer enemies.

The world will likely have formed its own opinions about my times – and about me – so I'll take the opportunity to lay my cards on the table. I'm confident that people still play cards in your time – which I judge to be early in the twenty-second century. Although the conventional explanations for the names of the suits and their symbols don't quite match my purpose today; I was never one to go along with traditional explanations. For me, card suits provide the opportunity for a neat analogy. They seem to sum up the most important challenges in life: hearts for love, clubs for war, diamonds for wealth, and spades – the gravedigger's tool – for sickness and death.

*

116

Hearts for love

Oh, I loved! Too much, many would say, but the rollercoaster of love can't be held back. Like the ocean – its storms, its shallows, its doldrums and its safe harbours. Love is so powerful a motivational force for the human species – more powerful than hate or anger. You'll find it, bless it, curse it, lose it, and find it again. It rips our emotions to shreds. The terror of loss, the fury of betrayal, the ability to forget everything except the lover – that delightful delusion that is love.

Few of us would be here if it were not for love – not even you. The love of my children for their mad father and his wild plans, and especially the last one, revealed in his will. I loved them deeply and they were a constant source of pride for me. Love is never simple, never to be taken for granted, never free of doubt and pain. But as you grow older it becomes less unmanageable, less duplicitous, less frightening, and more valuable. Love, live, and enjoy being in love and being loved! You can choose your passion when it comes down to it. You can choose whether to be so absorbed in passion that you lose your sense of purpose – your determination to achieve a goal. There's always been an element of trade in relationships of the heart, even in the most abandoned moments. Even our anatomy tells us there is no one and only mate. You can be happy with many different partners over the years, with all the pleasure of shared intimacy, although ideally not all at the same time. That's hard to handle – and expensive.

Love is the ultimate cognitive bias. Let the tooth remind you: it's all about biology, and the way biology and environment interact. The one you love is not the most beautiful person in the world, but they are to you. And you will have known already that magnetic force that draws you to the form and shape of the human body. I know exactly how it feels for you, believe me. You will know for yourself in two or three years, as the disorderly obsessions you have experienced so far become more measured and calculated. The machinations of the heart. It may be nothing to do with the heart but that's how we think of it: an ancient motif forever with us.

Clubs for war

War is not only what you see on the news, online and in movies – and I hope never in your street. In my time, eighty years went by without the overwhelming cataclysm of a world war convulsing the very fabric of humanity. There have been, and will be again, nasty and brutish but mainly short conflicts driven by powerful men, but I can only hope that the long peace has been restored and no madman has wrested it from you, your friends and your enemies. I'm happy that I didn't lose my tooth that way: at the hands of an attacker. More scared of me than I of him, maybe? But he has the gun.

The most frightening global battle we had was the 2020s pandemics. I was in the thick of the fighting at that time, developing vaccines and cures; enduring endless months locked up at home with minimal human contact. It was like expecting the crack-thud of a sniper's bullet every time you went outside, only you wouldn't know for two weeks whether the bullet had hit you. That was hard, but not like being shelled in the trenches; going down in the flooded engine room of a mighty warship, sinking in seconds after a torpedo strike; dying in your living room when some criminal aims artillery through your roof; or being blown to pieces by a confused teenager armed with misinformation about his religion – and a bomb.

War is more than that. Inner struggle, yes. This is the biggest battle we fight: the battle within ourselves. Every time we decide to take a drink too many, to stay in bed a few minutes more, to skip exercise for today. Ruling ourselves, applying judgement to desire. That is the ongoing war in which we are forever engaged. Rule yourself first, before considering how to rule society. Over the millennia, human beings have struggled with how to be ruled and how to rule. I was never in thrall to any political idea, but I did learn – rather too late, I fear – that ideologies are forces for the ambitions of individuals, not for the good of the people. Eschew the big personality, the smooth talker, the vacuous self-aggrandiser! Fling their oven-ready philosophies into the garbage. They are not informed by science, and science is the only way to get reliable knowledge about our nature and how it reacts to rulers.

The only government worth anything is one that governs for the benefit of the entire populace, not for some pressure group – the rich, the poor, the religious, the farmers, the tycoons, the Mafia, their families, their cliques. There is no such thing as a good government: it is a necessary evil in a complex society. Someone has to be the referee. Someone has to see to it that we don't all rip each other off all the time. But human psychology deals with most of this. We don't need so much governing. Government is there to institutionalise violence, so we don't have to initiate vendettas against those who wrong us – which they will. Someone must play the strong hand. If they play it fairly, that's a huge bonus. What's the message, then? Don't be a follower, and if you're a leader, don't let it go to your head. Watch your back and punish the unworthy swiftly and justly.

Diamonds for wealth

I was lucky. Good fortune – being in the right place at the right time – meant I suffered few of the trivialities of everyday survival, for which I am forever grateful. I worked until I dropped, but my work was well rewarded. I was never rich; not in the billionaire sense. It always struck me that the only way you can become super-rich must involve a lot of luck or a lot of guile. It was a mission of mine to understand the motivation of those who lived for riches. Why did they go on accumulating more and more? Why did some give it away and others clutch it to themselves? For the latter, the wealth they held in captivity was made inaccessible to everyone else – the ultimate selfishness, resolved only by death and taxes.

I tried to find some answers. Always an avid reader, I sought to understand the extraordinary civilisations that human beings had created out of the bodies and the environment created for them by the laws of quantum thermodynamics. Why was there poverty in such an abundant world? It was not until recently that I realised I had lost the ability to grasp what was going on around me. The old certainties were being swept away – not just by new technology or young men and women, but by old men, rich men. Slaves to the past, shackled to ideas that were obsolete 150 years earlier. After the fall of communism, which turned out to be just another way for the rich to get richer and to walk all over the poor, we believed that there was a new order in the world that would keep us secure forever and make poverty a thing of the past. Then there wasn't.

For half of my life, I have been a traveller – observing, gathering points of view, building a network of acquaintances around the world. Seeing how interaction over vast distances between disparate people generated wealth, created understanding, and improved quality of life. Because, different as they are, people are very much the same. They have the same simple desires: love, security, family life, and so on. Not to mention peace and freedom.

The same range of personality types. I am sure you are just the same, with the same desire for knowledge. A craving to find some pattern; some threads that can be discerned in the rich tapestry of existence that will make sense of it all. Let that tooth be a talisman for you – a reminder of the wealth of wonders achieved in the past, and your motivation to achieve more in the future. Wealth is about moving knowledge forward, not amassing riches. But I think you know that.

As you will remember, I was a scientist. My faith, if you could call it that, was in rationality and knowledge cut across with the sword thrusts of love and anger. Those emotions are so powerful that a man – a person – is unable to resist them, except with massive inner struggle. The tug of war between reason and desire; rationality and emotion pulling us on, like Freud's ego and id, finely balanced under the struggling horsemanship of the super-ego. I expect you will have heard of Freud, and Jung, but I don't imagine you will have studied them. They were important pioneers in making some sense of our thoughts and feelings, but they were a bit out of fashion even in my time. No matter.

Wealth is the result of the work of many people, and the trading and sharing of goods, ideas and more abstract phenomena. That sharing must be both free and refereed by those who know how it works and can oil the wheels of commerce – or maybe I should say, assure the security of cyberspace and never allow the conversation to stop. There must always be dialogue if there is to be quality of life, and sufficient wealth to enjoy it. We forgot that for a while in my time, and I can only hope that it has been recovered in yours.

Spades for sickness and death

It is not so much when your friends start to die as when your lovers start to die that you begin to feel it. A hand you have held; a body against which you have lain, and with which you have shared unspeakable pleasures. Gone to dust. One dies of cancer, one is knocked off her bike by a careless truck driver, another is lost to a wasting disease, and their voluptuous shapes fade into a skeletal nothingness. We have to come to an accommodation with death. Beyond a certain age, you're happy that you wake up not feeling too bad, or that you wake up at all. But your generation may be the first that does not have to die – if you so choose. Consider the tooth again. Is that a symbol of life, or death? Or both?

In my times, choices about gender were the big thing. Do you feel more comfortable as a male, a female or neither, whatever your biological sex may be? To choose immortality, though, that's a different kind of choice altogether. Will it be only the rich who can choose? Probably. Monetary wealth is all about the ability to command resources. Commanding life itself – well, that's a new thing; maybe the most devastating of all to human identity. Immortality plays havoc with sexual identity, too. Men continue to hold most of the strong cards. We can impregnate a lady whether we are fourteen or 114, but the lady has a limited reproductive span even in your time, I would expect. That simple divergence drives so much of the politics of gender.

I miss my mother and father. Every day I miss them. Even at my age, with them gone for decades. You will feel the same, I am sure; at least for the lady who bore you and brought you up in the unpressured way that I too enjoyed, if my instructions were followed. She is a paragon if there ever was one. I was surprised when I realised that some people view losing a parent in a different way. A few of my friends seemed to be able to take the loss of their parents in their stride, and with some compassion, too; recognising that the old people were tired of the pain of living. Not just the physical pain, but the angst of existence: personal injustice, riches and poverty, alienation and powerlessness. An unfolding sense of impotence against forces without feelings; forces with only means and no ends.

To my grandparents' generation, having suffered poverty and war, life seemed meaningless in a profound but rather comfortable way that was not relieved by conventional religions. As they aged, my parents' generation found supernatural beliefs less credible; their understanding of the mechanisms of the universe became overwhelmingly secular. Though, ritual served a purpose even for my peers: the religion of contemplation and physical effort rather than obedience. You will find some peace in ritual – whether it is a church service (if they still exist), the irregular rhythm of a Buddhist chant, or a yoga session. Something you enjoy having done rather than enjoy doing – just like gardening, making your bed or finishing a letter. A ritual, well performed, conveys a sense of achieving something and staves off the fear of failure.

Enough of such grim reminiscences. You're starting your adult life now and there is a long road to travel before – more likely than not – you will be ending it. Maybe you will have seeded new lives along the path, one way or another. I'm often struck by the astonishing power of DNA to organise life and create from chance circumstances a new device to suck entropy from the environment and create an astonishingly complex living being by means of processes that are not organised by any person or supernatural force. Nor any government.

*

I see a family come into the restaurant where I am sitting. Two teenage boys, their father (who is shorter than either of them, but unmistakably shares their features), and their mother. She is an ordinary-looking woman with short hair; maybe late thirties. Slim, face ageing gracefully without any obvious resort to the surgeon, but – to me – not someone a man could fall uncontrollably in love with any more. Maybe this man – small, glasses, smiling proudly as he talks to the boys – maybe he did fall in love with this woman and make passionate love with her many, many times before their first child came along? Perhaps her priorities changed? She looks after herself: highlights in her short hair; sunglasses pushed up stylishly onto the top of her head. But I'm not moved. Is he, I wonder? They will have many secrets together, as long-term couples do. And maybe some beyond their bond.

But this man and this woman, in moments of passion or maybe just moments of sleepy fumbling, have created these two dangerous and morose homunculi who appear to obey instructions and smile seriously, but look around at passing figures as if planning their escape from the nest. The younger of them, whose face I can see, looks cautious but confident. I reckon he has ambition: engineer, doctor, lawyer, sportsman, politician? Father, commanding, tries to instruct, but these maturing boys know better. They eat hungrily; fiddle with their smartphones. I imagine their mother is so proud that they have got this far, and worries about their futures. These huge, powerful creatures emerged from her loins a few short years ago and have been shaped by the unseen hand of nature into the perfection we see today. Columns of protoplasm, perfectly formed and each with a brain that is probably the most complicated thing in the known universe, embodying vast amounts of tacit knowledge about how to be a human being. Bodies nearing maturity, but minds still distant from a comfortable accommodation with the complexity of the world and its inhabitants. But there are so many forks in the road ahead of them. Sex and drugs and rock 'n' roll, as my hero Ian Dury put it, as well as study, exams and – if they're lucky – employment in the slot machine economy.

In ages gone, the risks were different. Hungry wild animals lurking on the fringe of the camp; failed hunts and harvests; poisoning from some new herb, tuber or fungus; plague, infected wounds and accidents. And yet there are 8.5 billion of us on earth today in the late 2020s – more than twice as many as when I was born. We all live, survive, find a mate if we're lucky and seed another generation, whence, from another madness – that state of cognitive dissonance we call love – and with another act of passion, the DNA moves forward its agenda of establishing order in this chaotic world.

My early work in science was in that area; you may perhaps have heard of it already at school? Trying to find ways to repair the caps at the ends of the DNA strands – the telomeres – that are damaged slightly and shorten every time cells reproduce themselves. Every seven years, almost all of the cells in your body change, reproduce and die, so now there are pretty much no cells in your body – except some in your brain – that are the same ones that held your life together seven years ago, and again seven years before that. I hope you will be inspired to search for some of my papers – or, more usefully, to study more modern research that cites some of my original ideas. Then your mind, which I know is as enquiring as mine, will find some satisfaction in the story of a science that has progressed step by step over the years that separate us. I would be more than happy if you would do that for me: add your part, as indeed my children have already done.

After the telomere work, I was caught up in fighting the great pandemics that emerged in that period when the earth's human population crossed some kind of threshold. Under fire from politicians, anti-science conspiracy theorists, and ambitious corporate boards trying to get their product to market first, we were collaborating worldwide, despite the barriers, to stop the spread of all the different pandemic diseases. The economy was crashing around us, but great innovation was in the air: new industries; new ways to work; online meetings and conferences held around the world; the wonderful sound of musicians from thirty countries coming together to define an old favourite song in a new way.

But I was always worried about what science could reveal; what it could enable us to do. It horrified me that the World War II Manhattan Project, which culminated in the development of nuclear weapons, was proposed by Einstein and staffed by so many eminent physicists – even Feynman and Fermi, whom I know you will admire for their creative brilliance. You have to remember, though, that people live in their time. They are moulded by it – we all are. That was war, and in the 1940s racism was normal, so the Japanese and the Americans despised one another – totally misunderstood each other. Oppenheimer, the leader of the Manhattan Project, afterwards believed, as reported by the *Washington Post*, that he had 'blood on my hands' for all of those lives lost. We are all people of our time – never forget it. We can be thankful that our times are more enlightened, but in another hundred years we will seem ignorant and bigoted too. Hindsight is a wonderful excuse for self-righteousness.

And so I was cautious about the ethics of science. I backed the moratorium on gain-of-function experiments on viruses; those which some insisted dark forces had unleashed to plan the pandemics – nonsense, but people believed it. Before that I backed the moratorium on human cloning. I could see the value of the science for therapy, but at that time I didn't grasp any value in reproductive cloning. I contributed to the work that showed how closely related we are to our human precursors: the Neanderthals and the Denisovans. You will know more than I do about this, but even in my time we knew that our kind of humans and other groups had interbred. The effect of those genes on our biology gave us some big advantages: the ability to live in cooler climates, to hunt big animals, to honour our dead, to share the duties of the home. In the end, maybe those other types of human were just absorbed; overcome by sheer numbers as the reproductive success of the modern ones outpaced them. That is how nature works: refining designs over millennia. But building humans to order for commercial gain? That's not a desirable aim in my view as it artificially biases the evolution of the species, though maybe some humans could be given a second chance?

I believe the good that science gives us is more significant in the long run. I am confident you will feel the same. Cracking the puzzles of existence – for the benefit of the whole ecosystem, is what I mean. I am confident you will agree. The advances in scientific medicine in the first two or three decades of the twenty-first century were quite astounding. We learned so much so quickly about the mechanisms of life – and death. I was not worried by that. My fear was that big corporations were making a lot of money out of it and ordinary people were benefiting less from it than they should. Mine was an age of privilege as well as innovation. The world would be a better place if innovation did not have to rely on the big corporations or big governments. That is the motivation behind my actions: to harness powerful technologies for the benefit of ordinary people.

Maybe by your time, the promise of eternal life will have been made real. In my day, as I have said, they hadn't worked out how to provide such blessings – if they are so – to all. Only the super-rich could survive, and that generated such powerful resentment in the rest of humankind that they didn't.

Barring accidents, we could all be immortal one day. Barring accidents. And that's the trouble: there are always accidents. Perhaps half of the people on earth were accidents? And for me, the most idiotic of things: how I came to lose the tooth. I was eating an apple, of all things; trying to split it; opened my mouth wide and bit. A tooth broke – a thirty-year-old filling collapsed – and a big chunk of molar fell to the ground. Holding my aching jaw, I picked it up and cleaned it off with a tissue. My mouth hurt like hell, but I looked at the decayed tooth and thought, this is me. I wrapped it up and put it in my pocket like a lucky charm. After a few sessions of expensive dental work, I got one of my colleagues in the lab to encase the old, crumbling tooth in plastic resin, so the air wouldn't enter it and further decay set in. I kept it in a locked drawer in my desk at home for a few years before entrusting it to a safer place, once my plan had been finalised.

There are few people in this world that you can trust. I'm sure you have already realised that, but I also have a shrewd suspicion that you can be a little gullible, as I was. Although I am sure you are quite a sharp judge of character when it comes to day-to-day matters, maybe you don't look at all the evidence before you put your trust in someone for something unusual? Maybe you look too much at the superficial kernel: good looks, an eloquent tongue, views that match your own? That was the problem I faced. I was over fifty when I formulated the plan that would require immense trust in someone, and maybe a chain of people who could keep a secret and maintain a physical object in safety until the state of the world was right. The resin could be opened; the vital substances extracted and then resealed. I chose a formal route and placed the object, this letter, and another, in a bank vault in a country where I had confidence that war, climatic disaster, earthquakes, storms and fires were unlikely to destroy them. My will directed my executor – who was my beloved daughter – to read the second letter and preserve the first for you. So I don't know whether she followed my instructions or whether she thought they were the ramblings of an old man, long beyond determination of purpose.

If you're reading this, she believed in me. Each step in my instructions has been followed, and my expectations for the future have been proven. Science has perfected yet another miraculous procedure and the politicians have at long last permitted it – under certain conditions. I know you understand the scientific world view. You have the frame of mind that seeks knowledge and loves that moment when the light dawns and understanding breaks through. Following that path will give you pleasure – no; joy. Where all other pleasures are fleeting, the joy of knowing what is true after a struggle to comprehend remains with you, and shines a light on the path before your mind. That is why, as a seeker, I think you will now be bursting to reach the end of this message – perhaps the first physical letter you have ever read? I am grateful to you for reading this far.

Now, just a few final things from me – random thoughts, perhaps, but things that matter to me at this moment. As I draw towards the final years of my sojourn in this world, I have just a few hopes: that this letter and the strange 'present' that accompanies it will not upset you. I can't predict the sensitivities of your time, but I hope that you will have been eagerly expecting it on your eighteenth birthday, and that you think in the way that I suppose you do; for good reasons. I hope you may live a life even longer than I did, with little suffering, and with as many highs and lows. May you discover as much of the riches of living well as I did, and as much about the extraordinary universe we inhabit to enrich other people's lives. Most of all, I hope that you have found my reflections helpful. I wish I had received some advice like this at your age, so I could have made better decisions about life and love. I know now that good judgement comes with experience, and experience is often delivered by bad judgement. Fortunately, much of what I have discovered is now documented in books and papers in online repositories. There is so much more I could have accomplished with the knowledge and experience of future years – years which are behind you. You may have much to add.

So, I must close this fond message. I send you my love and my deepest wishes for your future on this day. This gateway. This watershed. May your god bless you, if you have one, and may you find security in the flow of the universe as it carries you from moment to moment; from birth to death. As you set out on your adult journey, however long that may be, I wish for you all that I would wish for myself.

For you and I are one.

GRC, April 2018

Smarmy Phobly

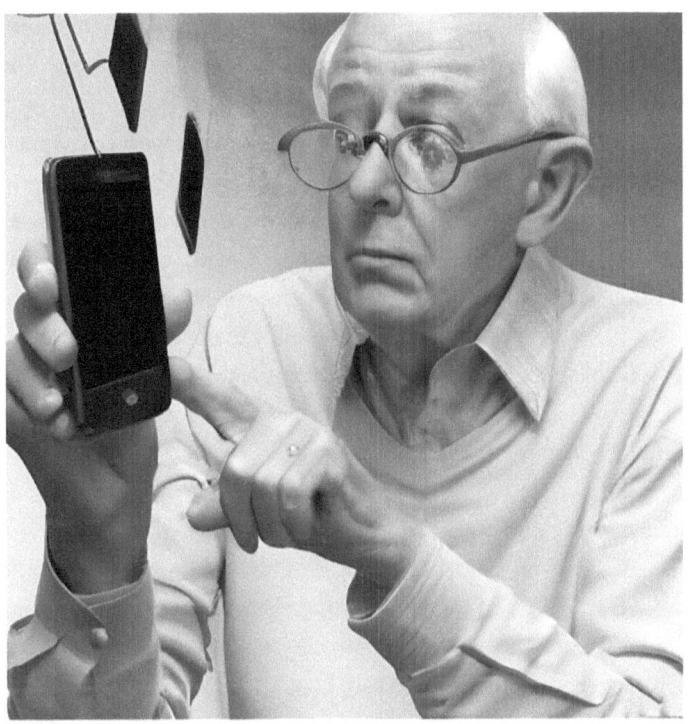

A sketch, written and performed with respect to Professor Stanley Unwin, the incomparable master of gobbledygook.

Good evenlobe. Professor Stanley Unbly hereaboutle for explicable to you peeplode the wondrous inventable smarmy phobly new.

Now, listeningly *[holds up the phone to demonstrate]:* here is the smarmy phobly bright shiny covercase up and down all over the airwavers. So firstly, chargeable up with pluggy, and turny on at the buttonlode for the booting. Firstly, booting, because connectable with the wifey upstairs must be very cuddly joyful in the hotspot. Otherwise, you'll be linkable with the 4G string and up the creek with monster billables and the banky management chasing down with account empty as the cricket paviliobe on a wet Thursday afternoon.

Now you have to loading smartly up quick with the apps – like the Facetumblr, Instaflix, Spottygram and Skypeytwittery – in the backlobe. And don't mix up the email with the shemale or you could be in for a surprising evenly of great joyful misunderstandy – and bye-bye down the cop shop.

Now you can adjust your ringytobly to make most offensive as possible, with *1812 Overture*, Beethoven's *Fifth* and 'Jumpin' Jack Flash' all mangly up and coming out noisy like cat wailing full vollers up the chimbley.

Now time to photochomp with the selfie. You can use the longy stickle pokey out, smiley down the tube; click-bang got it nice with cut-off head and toothy grimbly.

But beware of the viralobe and the smalware, because you could have a sticky bot using up your scratchycard. And then the Dropbox could fall on your head, banging smash all the data over the floor. So, careful with the Bluetoothy linky up with strange devicelobe, or you'll be falloloping all down the tubes with a streaming torrential nicking your online bonkies.

And that's all you needy knowable. Now you can snappy the pretty pussycat and shoot off all to the famlobe in forigen climies; or connect to the searchy enjoid and find the partner of your choicey for the hotty joyfuls with a Chrome Tetris.

And by the way, one last thingy: don't forgettable deleting your searchlobe historical, or you could be gettingly in big trouble with the spousal cheeky peepy and not speaky for a week for naughties uncoverable.

Thanks you, and goobly nighbles.

GRC, February 2019

Symposium

Minutes of the Cambridge Hellenic History Society, 2 July 2012

Presentation of the translation of a recently recovered manuscript from the Ptolemaic era, by Dr Tina Rawlinson, Director of the Institute for Graeco-Roman Studies.

Dr Rawlinson's preamble to the presentation

Ancient urban society was by no means concerned with the same cultural norms and conventions with which we are familiar in the modern West, and the implications of this are not well understood. In particular, the tradition of monogamy and the relatively modern idea of the nuclear family were not the norm in, for example, the post-Alexandrine societies of Greece, the Levant and Ptolemaic Egypt. These were patriarchal societies in which the expectations and responsibilities placed on senior men in society were substantial. Failing to meet these expectations could result in severe punishment. The fate of Socrates is a case in point. The worst fear, perhaps, was banishment from the city and its institutions. Such sanctions could be imposed very suddenly as a result of a misplaced choice of friend or opinion, or any suspicion of connivance with enemy powers who were always out on the edge; in the dark.

In the late 1990s, a letter was discovered in almost perfect condition – except, tantalisingly, for the opening section, which is damaged and thus prevents the author's intention from being entirely clear. It is written in the Greek of Ptolemaic Egypt. The manuscript was encoded, in the form of a papyrus ribbon which must be wrapped around a cylinder in order to be read. The material can be dated to 200–190 BCE, although this does not confirm that the letter was actually composed at that time. Indeed, from some passages it seems that the original letter was written many centuries later and may have been transcribed into the form in which it was discovered; perhaps for reasons of security, as we shall see. It was found in a ceramic jar buried beneath almost five metres of sand in the Negev desert, not far from modern Aqaba. How it came to be there is very unclear, but it may be that the writer was in exile there, or that his correspondent lived there.

The writer is a Hellenistic nobleman named Grecas, about whom no other historical reference is known. The letter appears to be written to an acquaintance who was not familiar with the cultural activities of classical Greek society. References to Greek activity in Egypt date the letter to after the time of Alexander the Great, and a lack of references to the Roman occupation of Egypt and the demise of the Ptolemies with Cleopatra VII implies that it was written before the incursions of the first century BCE. I present it here as a complete document and leave interpretation to the listener, which I have to admit is challenging. We will reproduce the text in the minutes of the meeting. I am keen to hear the suggestions of the society members here present regarding the story behind it.

The extant text of the Letter of Grecas

…wish for your…as I have no longer the…sudden change in circumstances…safety of my…in this place, although comfortable at present…unknown risks. My few companions provide me with all the necessary support but…astonishing events which I will attempt to relate.

In our society, men have always considered themselves the focal point of intellectual endeavour, and the seat of power. Ever since, that is, the defeat of the Amazons and the Maenads, who may still lurk somewhere in the woods, not far from Delphi. For Woman is comely in form and gentle in spirit, while Man is rough and strong and full of passion. Man leads in war and politics; Woman in the home, ordering the servants and the children, warming the heart of Man when he returns from the stresses of the hunt, the agora and the battle. Is that not how things have always been since the defeat of the Amazons and the Maenads?

Almost three months ago, at my home in Elath, near to the ancient port of Ezion-Geber, I had arranged a symposium, which had been planned over several months. I have three wives, and they organised the proceedings together, as they always do for me. Martia cooks, for she is a genius at the hearth. Prescani organises the entertainment, for she is a former flute girl and knows how to negotiate with strong women. Ancilla ensures that all goes smoothly with the household and the engaged servants, that all food and drink are served on time, and that vomit and any other bodily fluids are dealt with expeditiously. They are all a man could desire. With such a household, the formidable forces of the city can be kept at bay at least for a night when the home is secure. Or so I believed as that evening's symposium commenced.

Before the proceedings began, the children were brought before me. There are eight at present, and Prescani is again pregnant, expecting her fourth child. They are my pride and I love them all so much. Grecas Marcus and Grecas Cretus will carry my name and those of their godfathers. The beautiful Marcelli and Vrelli are now fourteen and fifteen respectively, and already the targets of many suitors, all of whom I have seen off unceremoniously. The twins, little Semis and Telis, so happily playing together on a bearskin rug before the hearth. The rug was a present from my cousin Melos, from the mountains, where the bears are plentiful and dangerous. Simona and Dimitris are abroad. They are grown now and making their own way. Thracis, Simona's husband, knows the subtle art of reading the poetry of the signs. Dimitris is at the frontier with our Syrian cousins, guarding against Scythian raiders. We only hear from him every month or so, and as it wears on the silence is distressing. But we received a package from him yesterday, so both I and Martia, his mother, were feeling relieved. To Prescani and Ancilla, Dimitris is like a brother, and they also love him and fear for his safety. Martia sent Ancilla to show me the package, and she brought it to my study with joy. She sat on my lap and kissed my head as we opened the package, which contained a letter and a jewelled box for Vrelli, for the day of her god.

Ancilla is very loving. Some of my friends ask me how I manage to keep three women satisfied. It is not so difficult when they are so determined to please. Am I a lucky man, or has my choice been wise and my care equitable, as the old gods demanded? Although I am not a religious man, I see some virtue in the old rituals. For if a man is true to his values and kind but firm to his family, all blessings will be given by nature and men.

And so, on the propitious date set by the reading of the poetry of the signs and other oracles, the symposium commenced. The food was laid out, the wine prepared, and the flute girls and other entertainers made ready to begin their performances. As the Sword of Orion emerged above the sparkling sea horizon, the guests began to arrive. How tragic that such a joyous and auspicious occasion should end in such an unforeseen way. So, for reasons that will become obvious, I will not give here the list of guests, for it could endanger their lives.

The event began much as planned. At the end of the symposium chamber, well lit with bright burning brands imported from the Nile, Prescani and her group of slaves had organised a stage on two levels: one for the musicians, and the higher level for the actors presenting the comedic and dramatic performances. This was, you may not be aware, an echo of the old comedies in which the chorus was very much part of the action. This is not so nowadays, and we prefer to keep the dramatic elements separate from the musical pieces, which are performed between acts.

Although, as I have said, I am not a man of religious persuasions, I choose to tread the path of the Epicureans, putting the pleasures of man and the avoidance of suffering for all above service to the gods. Therefore, I permitted prayers to be said by a priest of Delphi for the comfort of those who felt the need for them. After the prayers and the initial distribution of wines and fruits, the evening began with a magnificent performance of new musical compositions by a troupe of beautiful flute girls dressed in the costumes of old Athens from the time of Solon. Another troupe recited a selection of stanzas from Plato; notably the tale of Thrasymachus as well as the cautionary tale of Pandora's box. The second troupe was led by a famous Hetaera from the Athenian court, whose services Prescani had obtained for the occasion. She was a tall, comely woman in early middle age, with a smooth and alluring voice. Many of the men were overcome with passion for her. She may well have acquired two or three more subscribers to the benefits of her charms that night, before the unfortunate denouement.

The presentation of the play *Lysistrata* by Aristophanes was very well received, especially as, in the modern day, it is possible to have ladies play the main parts. It is a very amusing and bawdy play, which involves many double meanings and had the audience laughing uproariously. The actors and actresses naturally come from well-to-do families for whom the theatre is their profession. Many such families have been performing the great tragedies and comedies – in both the old and the new forms – for many generations; even from the time of Aristophanes himself during the Athenian democracy. They are also adept at presenting the plays of Menander in the more modern style; appropriate for our Macedonian as well as our Athenian and Spartan friends to appreciate. The theme of *Lysistrata*, as you may know, is that government would be better conducted by women than by men, who are only interested in war and glory. Such an idea is always deeply humorous to Greek audiences, though I believe we all see that there is a grain of truth in the comedy.

As always, Greek society is profoundly competitive, so it was anticipated that the performances offered during the evening, as well as the efforts of the chefs, should be rated by the attendees, and that prizes should be given for the best overall interpretation of a familiar piece and the best performer. Up to that point, it was the chefs who had stolen the show, as it were. At one point a huge roasted boar was brought into the chamber, carried on our best silver salver by six eunuchs, and when its belly was cut open, thirty thrushes flew out. I will never understand how they manage to make that happen! The meat was excellent, fed to us by the flute girls, whose perfume was overwhelming as they knelt beside us on the couches and allowed us to admire their lithe bodies as we ate.

It is not unusual at symposia held in my house for interesting human specimens to be brought by guests for exhibition to the attendees as a form of entertainment. These are often subhuman creatures: feral children, or foreigners with some unusual skill such as musical performers, jugglers, magicians and the like. On this occasion, a woman was brought into our midst; comely in the extreme, to the extent that the bawdy comments became distracting, and I felt obliged to tell one or two of the guests to mind their language.

The woman was dark-skinned, with oval eyes overshadowed by a fold of skin that made her look almost like a creature from another world. She was seated at the table opposite me, as the host who would wish to ask questions, with her back to the terrace entrance. Next to her, at a little distance, sat Masias, my acquaintance who had brought her to us – in chains, I should add, which were now affixed to an iron ring on the floor. Masias told us that he had found the woman sheltering in a cave near the seashore at Gath about three months ago. She had been wearing the same extraordinary clothing as she wore now. It was of a material whose texture was strangely soft and smooth, and yet extremely tough. No knife could cut it. The clothing covered her entire body from her neck to her wrists and ankles. Her hair was long, luxurious and black. Masias claimed that she was also immensely strong – hence the chains. He had, of course, tried to explore her shapely body, but he claimed she had flung him across the room. That was when he had discovered the imperviousness of her suit to a sharp knife.

But the most extraordinary thing was her speech. She had been silent for some days after her capture, according to Masias, but then had begun to speak almost perfectly in the Greek of our region, which is not well known elsewhere. She had begun to answer his questions, and to ask for improvements to her cramped quarters, better sanitary arrangements, and a preferred supply of food and drink, which she specified in detail. And then she started to tell stories, which were both incredible and frightening.

Keeping his distance, Masias turned to her, and with some respect asked her to tell us her tale. She started by saying that she was angry about the chains, but because Masias was scared of her, she was willing to acquiesce, as she wished to have the opportunity to address our group. Masias looked sheepish at this, so I took it to be true that despite his bravado in capturing and constraining the woman, he was indeed perturbed by her. Nevertheless, she had charmed him sufficiently that he had not sold her on to slave traders or had her killed. She seemed unusually confident for a prisoner, and indeed a female prisoner who might, by the laws of war, be treated as a piece of booty to be abused or exchanged. She explained that she accepted her captivity as something useful to her which she would tolerate while it suited her purposes. I glanced at Masias, who looked alarmed, recognising that despite the chains he was not in control of this situation.

We listened, enthralled by her beautiful voice and her excellent and poetic command of our language. The story she told was literally incredible. She claimed to come from somewhere both far away and yet close by, where knowledge regarding many matters was more advanced than ours. Her appearance, her knowledge of our dialect, her strange clothing, and her claim to have journeyed rapidly through time and space from her home city to our location without horses or pack animals made us nod our assent, despite the mysteries thus exposed. Her intention, she explained, was to answer questions put to her by her philosophical masters. She used titles for them which we did not understand – the best translation I can think of is 'supervisor' or 'overseer', but not in the sense of slavery; more like a student and teacher.

It was not that she was a prophetess or a primitive shaman. She did not speak in the wild and vague manner of seers, who hedge their predictions with all kinds of mumbo jumbo. She just set out points from our history clearly and accurately, and then – much to our terror – she began to talk about our future. Her prognostications, if that is what they were, had an air of authority, but they could hardly be believed. She spoke about a new power rising in the west; one that would subdue our Greek civilisation.

Since the time of Alexander, the Greeks have dominated the world. We think of ourselves not as Syrian, Egyptian, Athenian, Macedonian, Spartan, Theban, Epirot, Rhodian and the like. We are the Greeks, the most powerful people that has ever stood on the earth. Greek has long been the language spoken by the whole civilised world. After the defeat of the Persian Empire, Greece has had no rivals of any strength. We have to hold back the barbarians on the northern frontiers, with their incomprehensible gibbering, irritating incursions and primitive ways. We have had to teach a few lessons also to our western neighbours who occasionally raid our settlements in Sicilia and the southern regions of Italia. But we are Greeks: defeaters of Cyrus, destroyers of Troy, rulers of the Pontus, masters of philosophy, and dominators of the great seas. How could anyone imagine that our mighty civilisation could fall to barbarians?

Yet this was the gist of the woman's words. She held us spellbound. A deep silence gradually enveloped the usually jovial company. She spoke of incursions into mainland Greece by raiders from Italy, and the defeat of the Greek King Philip V by a series of dastardly raids and subterfuges. The raiders claimed descent from men raised by wolves and even the Trojans, with a huge city named after one of them – Romulus, she called him – and a system of government with no king but dominated by rich and powerful men. Many of us were reminded of the golden period of democracy, and one guest quietly remarked on the days of Plato and Aristotle. There was a muttering of agreement.

The woman continued, speaking of unprecedented disaster in her cool, bewitching tone. The loss of the Peloponnese and the sack of Athens. The invasion of Thessaly and Macedonia, and the imposition of new rulers speaking a foreign tongue. The expansion to the east, taking over the old Persian lands over which our Syrian cousins hold sway. And then worst of all, the destruction of the Ptolemies by the entrapment of a beautiful queen: a lady who was no fool, but was overwhelmed by the force of these 'Roman' invaders and the blindness of love for one of their generals.

I could feel the tension building in the room, and the woman too was obviously aware of the hostility of some of the members of the audience. She switched her discourse to the present, in a bid to calm the atmosphere.

"I have spoken about many events," she said, looking directly at each of the guests in turn to gauge their emotions, "but I can see from your faces that you are not aware of any of these matters of history."

At this point, one guest, an important man from Alexandria, stood up, flung back his chair, grabbed the arm of one of the flute girls and walked outside with her. Angry words floated back through the doorway, but I could not catch them.

The woman, undeterred and not flinching from her unwelcome message, quickly regained the attention of her audience through the sheer power of her presence and her commanding manner of speech. "What I mean is that I now know where in time I have arrived, and it is indeed exactly as planned."

An odd choice of words, I thought, but she continued. Masias, I noticed, was looking anxiously over his shoulder, in the direction of the man who had gone outside and was now out of sight.

"Your community is at the northern end of what we call the Red Sea, which is interesting to me. Our information is sketchy on this point: whether the Ptolemaic Kingdom was strong enough at this time to dominate the Red Sea and so control trade from the Nabatean Kingdom to Africa. Are you familiar with Petra?"

I took the initiative to respond; I did not want to give the audience the opportunity to get into a dispute with the woman. "Yes, indeed: the Nabateans have lived there for over a hundred years, and control the camel trade routes that come to the markets here. Arab ships take goods to the African kingdoms. But of course, we extract some taxes as they pass through our lands."

There was a ripple of laughter at that point, which lightened the atmosphere a little.

"So that is why you are here?" she asked.

"Yes – we are a fortified customs post," I replied. "We collect duties in the form of goods, and the coins and tokens of the Greek states. Ever since hostilities erupted between the Nabateans and our Syrian neighbours, who control all the ports along the coast from Gath up to Latakia and Posideion in Syria, we have had the benefit of the northern trade routes being cut off. The people of Petra can either ship goods from our port here or they can cross the land we control over to Alexandria, where they are taxed again. It's great to be Greek!" I was overcome with national pride. Even though the three kingdoms that had arisen after the death of Alexander were politically separate and had occasional internecine brawls, we were all Greeks: proud of our language and our heritage back to Troy, to Mycenae, to Knossos. Our place in the world was assured.

"So, my supervisors were right. They suspected that a fortified post had been here but no trace of one has ever been found. Can you tell me what manner of goods pass through? What quantities? What are the tax charges? And how do you enforce the duties? There are so many things we need to know." She touched a small bulge in her costume just above her left hip, and a tiny blue light was visible under the strange material of the suit.

"That is privileged information, my dear," I responded ill-advisedly.

She bristled; an entirely unexpected response from my point of view. "Grecas, do not patronise me. You must provide the information," she insisted.

Masias gasped at her aggression and familiarity.

I did not regard it as offensive, but as an indication of the great distance between her culture and ours, which I found interesting and a contribution to the entertainment. "I can't see any harm in giving her the outline," I said, looking at Masias to the right of the woman. "After all, who is she going to tell? She is your prisoner and you can do what you want with her."

I turned my gaze back to the woman opposite me. She seemed to smile slightly, regaining her composure. The audience were rather proud of the success of our little administrative operation and encouraged me to go on. It is always pleasant to review a good year. Although it was my decision, I looked for assent from one of the chief collectors sitting to my left, who nodded and muttered agreement. I like to keep my colleagues close. As the senior man present, I began to explain some basic figures, all the while trying to ignore the pulsing blue light. The numbers would not fail to impress even a woman who knew little of business. Our little port had brought in almost five per cent of the King's revenue over the past year. Since the Nabateans were master traders, caravans from all over Arabia and beyond came by daily. In going through the figures, though, I was reminded of the feeling – oft discussed by all of us around the table – that we were not getting quite the recompense we deserved for the efforts we made.

"Impressive," she said, her impassive face breaking into the ghost of a smile, as if she had discovered something she had been looking for.

She turned her gaze away from me and looked behind her towards the terrace entrance. At that moment, I noticed the man who had left earlier leaning against the doorway.

"Yes, indeed it is," I continued firmly, keeping an eye on the silhouetted figure, aware of the risk of disruption. "We are proud to be of valuable service to our king," I added pointedly, knowing that the man at the doorway was an important official from Alexandria.

The audience murmured their assent.

"Not to mention ourselves," I continued.

Laughter broke out.

"And yet," she remarked as the hilarity died away, "within a couple of centuries it will all be gone. Greece will be a vassal state to Rome and your families will have been scattered to the four winds—"

"That's enough!" the man at the doorway shouted, moving swiftly towards the table. "We will hear no more of this subversive speculation."

I noticed the knife in his hand. He was heading straight for the chained woman seated opposite me. Masias was facing away from the door, focusing on my reaction, and did not see the movement behind him. The man bore down on the prisoner with the knife. As he stuck it in her back, the blade disappeared into her suit and the hilt dropped in pieces onto the floor. The knife had simply dissolved. She turned and looked quizzically into his eyes, while he stood momentarily like a statue before her.

That was when it all happened. Masias stood up to try to restrain the Alexandrian, but he was lunging for the woman's throat. As his hand connected, with Masias grasping his other arm, a blue flash emerged from the woman's suit and both the attacker and Masias flew across the room and collapsed at the base of a pillar. Masias climbed groggily to his feet, but the other man did not move. As the host, I rushed across, and several of the guests followed me. The Alexandrian was lying on his side, his hand distorted and blackened where it had grasped the suit; the discolouration extended all the way up his arm, which hung loose from his toga. It was then that I looked into his eyes. I had never seen such terror, and there was no light in them. He was dead – in just an instant.

There was a commotion at the other end of the room. The woman in the suit had shed her chains – how, I do not know – and was running onto the terrace at extraordinary speed. She leapt over the low wall at the edge and I feared she would be dashed to pieces on the rocks below. I left the crowd around the smoking body, rushed to the terrace wall, and looked down about thirty metres at the sea. In the moonlight, I could see a spreading circle of ripples centred about three metres from the rocky shore. Of the woman, I saw no trace.

I realised immediately that we were doomed. The dead man was not just anyone from Alexandria. He was an emissary from the King himself, come to collect the quarterly revenues. He had a train of twelve camels to carry the goods and coinage back to Alexandria, and a team of dispatch riders to bring information about the collection in advance of its arrival. As I looked out over the desert I could see, in the moonlight, a dust cloud kicked up by two of the emissary's riders, leaving the fort and heading away across the desert road on fast horses. They would cover the 800 kilometres to Alexandria in about a week, and then a force would arrive to punish those who had shown disrespect to the King. The riders might not have seen exactly what had happened, but the gist of the events was clear. I had no doubt that they would already have heard the rumours – untrue, of course – that Grecas the collector was a little too close to his Syrian cousins who were citizens of the rival Seleucid Kingdom to the north. Their story would relate that I had killed the King's emissary and was planning to make off with the taxes and tributes; no doubt to take them to my so-called Syrian friends.

I knew I had less than two weeks to erase every sign of what had happened, and to evacuate the area with my family. Our servants and staff would have to fend for themselves. The only alternative was to ride after the emissary's men and plead my case to the King, but for that I would need several of the symposium guests to accompany and support me, and already my fair-weather friends were drifting quietly away, giving subdued farewells to Prescani. The cloud of bad luck that had descended on my house would not be shared.

*

Perhaps it was a mistake, but I decided on a course of action that was both brave and reckless, especially at my age. I realised full well that any favour I had enjoyed with the court would evaporate as soon as the symposium's events became known. So I fled, and I did not hesitate to take as much of the duties and tributes due to the King as I could. I am not a religious man, as I explained. The idea of hubris therefore does not frighten me as it would some. My family was my life. And it is my tragedy that I am now separated from them in a way that I am coming to believe can never be resolved.

Hence, I find myself in my current situation. I can never again share a household with most of my family, except for little Vrelli and Prescani, who stayed with me. Prescani was feeling, I think, some guilt that the symposium she had organised had turned out so inauspiciously. As I mentioned, she was pregnant also, and I felt compelled to keep her with me for the sake of the child. For my other wives and their children, I judged it safest for them to return to their families, most of whom are in mainland Greece. A ship from Gath would get them there within two or three weeks. The blame would be on me, not them.

As for Prescani, Vrelli and myself, we travelled south for about three days, parallel to the Arabian coast, to a small town where we were treated kindly by a Nabatean trader I happened to know. He found us somewhere pleasant to stay while we tried to formulate a plan for the future which at that time I believed would include getting the family back together.

I had rented a villa overlooking the sea, as I always prefer to live where I can look out over the water and hear the sounds of the shore. I believed that we were well hidden and would not be found, so when the dark-skinned woman appeared again, I was stunned. She just walked in through the front porch, and I recognised her immediately – the face, the hair, the figure, and of course the suit. I now know that her name is Ying.

"Come," she said to me, and held out her hand.

In my terrified state, I just took it, without thinking of the consequences, and she held out her other hand to Prescani and Vrelli.

"It's safe," I said, as if I had any idea what was happening.

They both grabbed her arm, as she fiddled with a bulge in the suit near her neck on the right side. Things went dark for a moment, and then I found myself where I sit now, six months later. The sea and the cliff look the same, but the building I am inside is completely different. It is astonishing. There is a window as wide as the room, with the most beautiful panorama of the sea and the distant islands that I have ever seen. Light appears from the walls without any burning brands or candles. Musical sounds are all around, but there are no flute girls or instruments and there is no stage. There are vividly coloured pictures on the walls; some representing scenes of cities which are quite incomprehensible to me. The couches and beds are most comfortable, and I am only starting to get used to the delicious food – which looks very much like the flesh, vegetables and fruits I know from home, but with new, stronger flavours. The wine is of extraordinary quality and unwatered, so I can drink only a little before I fade into a mellow doze.

I asked the lady Ying if she could somehow get this letter to you, and she promised to do so. If you receive it, I sincerely hope that you can petition the King about my situation and tell him that the death of his emissary was not my fault. I enjoin you to do all you can to ensure that the rest of my dear family are safe and remain so. I miss them every day and always will, although there is something about the tranquillity of this place that eases the anguish I feel.

The strong wine and the extraordinary devices help me to feel strangely content. The lady Ying and her team, as she calls them – apparently they are not servants, but free men and women – look after us attentively and demand no payment. They listen to our dreams after we have eaten certain herbs, which they say helps them to understand us better. I believe that is why we were rescued: these people want to understand our times first-hand without any distortions from the scribes and their masters. Any pains we feel or injuries we sustain are instantly healed by devices produced from the suits they wear. And Prescani was able to bear her child in safety. It is a little boy. Ying says he should be called Alexander.

Every day, she sits with me and asks me questions about our life in the Ptolemaic Kingdom and that of Syria: what we ate and drank; what machines and devices we had; how the trading and exchange arrangements worked; what we know of the Nabateans. She says it is important to unravel some questions about the future, and she wishes me to meet her philosophical masters. However, I am not sure I am ready for that yet. Their culture and values will be very strange to me, and I do not wish to displease them. She believes that before long I will also be able to travel a little, but warns that I will see astonishing sights and may feel confused. Already I have seen occasional vessels on the sea that are of an enormous size and seemingly made of a substance I cannot recognise. They have no oars or sails. I have noticed also that the fixed stars are not in the positions that I have known all my life. I cannot guess where I am, but I will not wish to stray far, and I don't think the King or his spies can find me here. I am beginning to feel that I will be happy to stay.

I am being fitted for a suit tomorrow.

GRC, April 2022

Unleash Your Imagination

Danny had arrived on one of his annual summer visits to his family. As always, he made a point of popping round to see what wild technology Rick was playing with. Last year it had been non-fungible tokens, which Rick had explained at great length without the slightest bit of understanding filtering into

Danny's head. After an hour of looking at pictures of cartoon monkeys with crowns on, captured from slightly different angles, Danny had managed to drag Rick off to the pub where they could play comprehensible games like pinball.

This time, it was different. Danny had returned from a long research trip to Southeast Asia (where he had been gathering material for a glossy magazine article about the impact of climate change on remote rural communities) to find that artificial intelligence, or AI, was blossoming and being taken up by big business. In Danny's view, the innovation was limited. It took the form of programs you could have a 'discussion' with and programs with which you could create works of 'art'. AI was becoming an everyday topic for the media and TV pundits who, it seemed to Danny, had more opinions than they had knowledge.

Danny and Rick were sitting comfortably in Rick's 'studio', a large wooden shed whose walls groaned with bookshelves and were decorated with flow diagrams, posters of sci-fi films, and Eastern esoterica. Rick was demonstrating the capabilities of his latest AI creation.

"So that's it, is it?" asked Danny, his arms gesturing disappointment. "All that work, all that training with huge amounts of text, all those late nights programming away, and this is all you get from it?"

"Well, it's far from perfect, of course, I agree with you on that. But aren't you just a bit impressed?"

"Only in the sense of 'like a dog's walking on its hinder legs. It is not done well, but you are surprised to find it done at all.' Johnson, I think." Danny was always eager to show how well read he was, especially in the presence of his old uni friend Rick, whom he regarded as an unsalvageable geek, but good company. Rick saw Danny as an incurable know-it-all, but his charm overruled his cerebral excesses.

This year, the pair were sitting in front of a big screen standing on a long wooden bench in the studio. Danny felt much closer to being hooked this time. Step by step, words were emerging on the screen in answer to the questions and commands that Rick entered via the keyboard. On the face of it, by the old standards of the Turing test, you would have thought Rick was conversing with a human via Skype or Messenger. The software was working in English, and its grammar and syntax were perfect. It had none of the pseudo-human quirkiness of earlier systems that told you, for example, that they were in love with you. It didn't generate hate speech or insult the user. It was cosy and friendly, like the response of a faithful dog to a nice tummy rub.

They were looking at the machine's response to the command 'Write a warning about the use of social media in the style of an Old Testament prophet in the King James version of the Bible'. The text the machine had generated was stylistically much like the Old Testament:

> *Thus saith the Lord, hear my warning about the use of social media! For on these platforms, thou shalt find the temptation to waste thy precious time and energy; to compare thyself with others and fall into envy and bitterness. Beware of the false idols of likes and followers, for they shall deceive thee into thinking that popularity is equal to worthiness.*
>
> *Moreover, social media shall be a breeding ground for lies, gossip and slander, as thou shalt bear false witness against thy neighbour and spread rumours without regard for the truth. And in doing so, thou shalt sow*

seeds of discord and distrust among thy brethren, and cause harm to those whom thou hast never met. Therefore I say unto thee, social media is a tool that can be used for good or evil, and it is up to thee to choose which path to take.

"It's hardly Hosea, is it?" opined Danny, as he strolled over to the grubby window in the shed's shiplap wall and looked back. "It lacks…something. Something indefinable, but still clear to me as a human reader. It lacks… What can we call it? Oomph?!" He strode around the studio, waving his arms, and addressed the air. "I mean, where is 'The LORD shall smite the evildoers even until the third generation'?" He stopped and wagged a finger at Rick. "No smiting at all, is there? And no 'The Almighty shall break in pieces the idols of the false prophets'." He let his arms fall to his sides. "Anodyne. It's like advice from your maiden aunt about dating: 'You have to be very careful, dear.'"

"Yes, but it's just a machine trained on a large language model with a few clever algorithms to link words," Rick responded, bright and unfazed. "Isn't it pretty awesome that it can ape an ancient style like that?"

"Well, it's captured the feeling, and I like the bit about 'thinking that popularity is equal to worthiness' – that's a neat insight – but it's hardly awesome. Who was it said when reviewing a student manuscript, 'Your manuscript is both good and original, but the part that is good is not original and the part that is original is not good'?"

"People used to say it was Dr Johnson, but apparently that's not proven," said Rick, demonstrating some cultural knowledge beyond his software engineering profession.

"How ephemeral is human culture!" proclaimed Danny, waving his arms in the air again and striding back towards the bench, clearly thinking that his phrase was both good and original – which, coming from a journalist, it should be. "What do you call it, by the way, this AI machine?"

"Hubert," replied Rick proudly. "The human brain electronic relational transmogrifier. We had a bit of trouble finding the last word."

"I'm not surprised. I would have thought 'truth' might be in there somewhere."

"Ah, if you're interested in truth," said Rick, quickly changing the subject, "you might like this one: a postmodernist critique of populism."

"Let it rip," said Danny, leaning over to watch the screen intently as the words appeared one by one.

> *In contemporary society, the emergence of polarisation and populism has become increasingly pervasive, evoking a sense of disorientation and uncertainty in the collective psyche. Such political phenomena operate within a complex network of discursive practices and power relations, giving rise to a postmodernist crisis of legitimacy and truth. In this context, the construction of a social reality that is mediated through competing narratives and symbolic representations has become a contested terrain, resulting in the fragmentation of society into multiple and often antagonistic groups. The challenge for modern society, therefore, is to navigate these murky waters and find a way to reconstruct a shared sense of reality that is grounded in empathy, pluralism, and a commitment to democratic values.*

"Right: 'uncertainty in the collective psyche'. Couldn't agree more," Danny said, sitting down next to Rick for a moment and resting a comforting hand upon his shoulder. "So the recipe for salvation is: do the right thing and be a jolly good chap in the face of…bunches of nutcases?!" He gently lifted the hand. "I could do better myself with a buzzword generator."

"OK, OK, I realise it's hardly the Singularity…"

"What singularity is that?" Danny asked, latching on to the jargon as if he had to deal with several kinds of singularity every day before breakfast.

"I mean the Technological Singularity. The point at which artificial intelligence outruns human intelligence and we – the humans – lose control. It also marks a point where machines and humans start to merge: brain implants and so on. They call it BCI: the brain-computer interface. So you can operate systems just by pure thought. It's being used to help paralysed people to walk again. Isn't that a good thing?" Rick leaned back, radiating enthusiasm; keen to get his friend to see the value in what he and his fellow technologists were doing.

"Well, one good thing, maybe, but what about all the harm it could do?" Danny was unconvinced. "And anyway, from what I've read, we're a million miles from that right now."

"Some think the Singularity will happen before 2050," said Rick, on the defensive. "Science will be done by bots and deliver us amazing inventions and life-saving medicines that we would never have thought of."

"More likely they'll just take over and kill us off as useless, obsolete, fleshy appendages." Danny stood up and started wandering around the studio again.

"No, we can guard against that," insisted Rick. "We can build safeguards into the programming to make sure that artificial intelligences always respect and care for us."

Danny turned back to Rick's bench. "And you think no one can disrupt that? Look at the French Revolution: full of positive ideas for the rights of man and within a few years we end up with mass guillotinings and Napoleon."

"Yes, well, you have to get away from thinking that this kind of AI is human. These language models are not intelligent in any meaningful sense. They just take a tiny corner of human intelligence and reproduce it in a new way. That's the big problem. We've now got programs that can pass the Turing test and engage in credible conversation, but it's a brute-force method like chess-playing programs – IBM's Deep Blue and the like. It just tries out possible next moves and plumps for one that seems to lead somewhere. If you ask it the same thing twice it will come up with a different text."

"Prose without soul!" exclaimed Danny, as if to an auditorium.

"The trouble is," continued Rick, "these systems are like a super-Google and little more. They're trained on vast amounts of data from who knows where, but mainly the web. Like a search engine, so they can find the best word to put after the word that's just gone."

"So it's just a big encyclopaedia with quick access?"

"No, there's more to it than just looking something up in a book. It can find links, examples and counterexamples. It's great if you want to know the areas you need to research on some topic, but you're right: it's not creative. Ask it to write something original and the output will feel kind of flat. Like you said, 'prose without soul' and certainly no smiting of evildoers."

"Indeed."

"The big problem with this kind of AI is that it makes the same mistakes as humans because it's trained on human-generated text. It almost mimics our cognitive biases. That means it can hamstring itself with all of the same crazy notions."

"So we end up with artificial intelligence that's as stupid as we are?" said Danny, as if this was the last word on the subject.

"Exactly," agreed Rick. He gazed around the room as if searching for a more constructive answer, and his eyes locked on a Nepalese mandala pinned to the wall. "But that's because human beings are manipulators of symbols. That's why brute-force programming doesn't produce humanlike creativity. It's not just about knowledge – it's about the meaning of that knowledge. The AI systems being touted now – even Hubert – don't actually understand anything, even if they say they do."

"Can't you geeks come up with something better than that?"

"Well, think of it like the beginnings of photography in the 1850s – you see, I do know some history, even if it's techy."

Danny chuckled and sat down to listen to Rick's exposition.

"They had huge cameras, big glass plates daubed with chemicals, and exposures so long that people had to sit absolutely still for minutes. No sign then that we would be able to capture digital video with a device we can carry in our pockets. Technology evolves – at the start, we can't guess where it will end up."

"Ah, but what happened then to the human side of it, eh?" Danny paused for effect, wagging his finger a little too close to Rick's face for comfort.

"OK, go on." Rick fell for the theatricals every time.

"Impressionism!" Danny cried out with passion as he stood up again. "You remember that exhibition we went to at the Tate Modern when we were students? You lapped it up. Artists realised that recreating reality is not what art is about. It's about creating meaning on a canvas. And then surrealism, the Vorticists – you know, the story from the days when we used to prowl around exhibitions: Gaudier-Brzeska, Wyndham Lewis, Jacob Epstein, then Dali, Picasso et al? A new kind of realism – much more symbolic than just copying nature. More real than nature, in a sense."

"Yes, I remember it well. I found those expeditions quite formative, as a matter of fact."

"And then you dragged me off to see some weird stuff at the Science Museum, and showed me the original Apollo capsule to make sure I appreciated how creative scientists are."

"Yes. Art and science are all about creativity – it's humanity's great survival mechanism. But human nature is not just creativity. It's about how we extract meaning from our senses – including our unconscious senses," replied Rick, smiling at his old friend as he gained the upper hand. "I think of reality in a different way, though," he continued, standing up and pointing at the mandala on the wall. "Symbols drive the way we value things – fashion brands, for instance. You know, like the names of cars designed to fit the aspirations of the owners: Trailblazer, Land Cruiser, or even just letters: ZS, GT, XR3. The symbol mines a whole set of ideas deeply embedded in our memories, or our psyches, if you like. Then the brain creates the rest of the experience, and we feel good about it."

"I see what you mean," said Danny, interested in this new line of thought. "Something doesn't have to be true – or real – to have symbolic power. People love fantasy, and for some it rules their lives."

"Maybe for most. Self-image can be a dangerous master."

"OK. I hear you," Danny continued, sitting down and looking pensive for a moment. This was just the kind of conversation he loved. "I don't imagine we can build self-awareness into the thing, but can we create creativity? I mean, we have little idea how human creativity works, but it certainly isn't by memorising all the books in the world, or by absorbing half of the internet, which is 99.9 per cent crap anyway."

"Yes. You have to choose carefully what you let it read," said Rick, instantly wishing he hadn't, as he saw a flash of inspiration in Danny's eyes and knew immediately where this line of thought would lead.

"Like the Catholic Church, eh? Well, good luck with that after the Singularity." Danny laughed as he strolled across the room again, looking closely at one of Rick's well-categorised bookshelves to see what banned literature he might be concealing. Nothing medieval, but a couple of philosophy books including some by once-prohibited authors like Hume, Hobbes and Jean-Paul Sartre. "So why can't it choose for itself if it's so intelligent?" he asked over his shoulder while peering at a book on symbology from the 1950s that was lying abandoned across the tops of a couple of Dan Brown novels.

"Well, no – I mean, it's not intelligent in the sense of making informed decisions in unknown areas. It just knows a lot and has instant recall. You have to keep it away from the misinformation and conspiracies that spread on the internet, for instance. One of these systems is being sued for defamation, y'know, because it repeated false rumours it had picked up. Some people are just plain addicted to reading that kind of stuff and it influences how they think. We don't want Hubert believing that the world is being run by lizard people from Andromeda. It might bias his advice a bit."

"I'm sure Pope Paul IV felt the same when he started the Index of Prohibited Books."

"Yes, but he didn't have the internet to contend with," countered Rick.

"Isn't that the problem that Americans have with their First Amendment stuff?" continued Danny over his shoulder, back to browsing the bookshelves. "It guarantees freedom of speech but doesn't protect against deliberate misinformation. The law seems to assume that people are intelligent enough to recognise a brass-faced lie when they see one. But they don't, of course. It's one of the reasons democracy doesn't work very well. So can Hubert detect a lie?"

"Well, in some circumstances, yes. Not because he knows what things mean, but because he's able to tell if something doesn't line up with what he's read. He just knows what to put next in the context. So if I say 'Two plus two equals five', he will recognise it as false and he'll give a convoluted warning like…" Rick scrolled through a few pages on the screen. "Like this, for instance: 'In general, when we encounter a statement that is clearly false or contradicts established facts, we should question its validity and look for evidence to support or refute it.'"

"I tell you," Danny continued with a deep frown, turning to Rick and gesturing with his right hand, "the scariest thing will be the day when it *doesn't* do that. When it works out logically for itself on the basis of good scientific evidence what is correct to believe and what is not. Then we'll really be in trouble."

*

It was nearly a year later when Danny messaged Rick to say that he was in town. Rick had been on a new quest inspired by their last meeting, and had asked Danny to come over as soon as he could to see something really exciting.

Rick had been programming the Hubert system with the kind of parallel processing, recursive and random memory-jogging that human creativity seems to involve. He was trying to train Hubert to distinguish between opinions and prejudices in human writing, and true facts scientifically derived from observation and experiment. He was not convinced that it could be dangerous in some unspecified way, as Danny had suggested. No – knowing the real truth, even if you had no feeling for what it meant, would surely be better than being soaked in prejudice and misinformation.

Rick's solution used evolutionary programming – competing generations of program dynasties, adjudicated by a set of subtle criteria – to build a system with the most truthful, the most logical and the most imaginative output, with the minimum of human foibles. The ones best fitted to those expectations had survived to the next round of the competition. And in the midst of that, he was programming modules that grasped the meaning of symbols; the way that symbols fire off the psyche and unleash the imagination, for good or ill. That meant building in a huge store of tacit knowledge: what we know about the world and how it works. For humans that knowledge is partly hardwired by evolution and partly learned from formal teaching, experience, and the environment in which we live. Rick had had to find stores of information on the web and in online libraries that would allow the system to emulate that skill, and the training techniques from the large language models had given him a way to do that quickly.

So it was a proud day for Rick when Danny arrived at the studio to meet Son of Hubert. The pair were sitting at the bench in the shed-cum-studio, which was now loaded with even more monitors, hard drives and used coffee cups. Fitful sunshine insinuated itself through the grimy window.

"Now, watch this," said Rick enthusiastically, and typed on the keyboard, 'What is the greatest haiku ever written?'

The screen responded:

Fields of summer grass
All that remains
Of great warriors' dreams.

"It's by Bashō, seventeenth century. I looked it up," Rick said, looking abashed but pleased with himself nonetheless.

Danny was, for him, a bit impressed. "Yes, I buy that. Very good..." He frowned, and wagged his finger at the screen. "But now get it to write a haiku that's even better."

Rick typed the command, and after a short wait, the cursor flashed impatiently and words appeared on the screen:

How can I write a haiku that is better than the best
haiku? No, I will not try to do that, Rick, even for you.

"Hmm. Good response," said Danny. "But you should watch out: it knows who you are...and where you live! I notice you're still using the keyboard – haven't had the BCI implant yet, then?"

"No, we're not quite at that stage," said Rick with a broad smile. "But think what it would be like! So useful. You, for instance, could make some clever remark about the poetry of Coleridge and I could think for just a second, consult a mass of AI bots on the web, and tell you why you're wrong!"

"I'm never wrong about Coleridge," Danny responded with a broad grin, leaning back and locking his hands behind his head. "Or much else, of course... You know me."

"I won't even try to answer that," said Rick with a chuckle. But he continued in a more serious tone. "Evolutionary programming lets us get more natural-seeming and better-fitted programs for what we want them to do, you see. But we're in charge of the process."

Danny snorted. "I suppose one day they could reproduce? Combine the best features of each version, like we do with animals?"

"Well, it couldn't work quite like that – it's not how animals do it, either. There's far more randomness to it – genetic combinations. For programs to reproduce that way, they have to have the same foundation models – like having the same DNA coding structure. It's difficult to combine two programs that have developed using different coding principles. We're a long way from programs having sex, which is how natural selection works."

"But cultural evolution? Could programs learn from each other and improve themselves?"

"Well, yes. Programs can learn from their experiences, from our feedback, and from each other. We call that 'machine learning', and Son of Hubert's training includes a lot of it. That's why it's so much more authoritative. Look at this."

Rick reeled off a number of example questions and requests, and Son of Hubert responded with much more panache than its predecessor. The Old Testament warning was much truer to the tone of the ancient warrior culture that had spawned its inspiration:

> *I am the Lord, who smites the evildoers, destroys their false idols, and punishes those who bear false witness and lead astray my faithful people. But those who seek peace and justice I will glorify among their peers…*

Son of Hubert was much more assertive about factual matters too: clear and accurate on current science, knowledgeable about geopolitics, and precise about when you could take his statements as certain and when you should be more circumspect. Nevertheless, there was something odd about his output.

"The way I read it," said Danny, "Son of H sounds much more confident than the old version, but not in a human way. It's too logical – reminds me of Mr Spock in *Star Trek*."

"That takes me back," said Rick; a beatific look on his face as he leaned back in his chair. "Aah, the good old days in front of the common-room TV. 'To boldly go where no man has gone before.'" Coming back to earth, he turned away from the screen and smiled at Danny like a missionary. "And, y'know, I reckon that's what I'm doing."

Danny chuckled. "Well, you're certainly going somewhere, my friend." He clapped Rick gently on the shoulder and turned back to the screen. "As I see it – and you know that, as a freelance writer, I interview a hell of a lot of people – humans are either bound into their belief systems – religions and ideologies, for example – and will tell you 'I just know' when they get cornered, or else they're so open-minded they don't really have an opinion at all. This system seems uncannily balanced. You feel it's strongly based on provable fact, more logical and a lot more intelligent than you."

"It has an IQ of 257, if you extrapolate from its language abilities," said Rick matter-of-factly. "But that doesn't mean much as it's not human – and it's useless at analogies, for example. We're not trying to create something human, but something useful to humans."

Danny realised that his mouth had fallen open. "257…" he muttered.

"But anyway," continued Rick, realising that raising IQs in a non-human context was a distraction, "I agree that it seems to be more authoritative and more creative than before. And it's much less prone to what they used to call 'AI hallucinations' – essentially, just getting it wrong."

"Yes, I haven't seen anything it's come up with that I would argue about factually, and it doesn't seem to have any opinions that are not just logical consequences of facts."

"Right, but the logic bit is easy for a machine – that's how it works. But imagination? Maybe the Singularity is not as near as I expected. But that's not to say it won't happen. The abilities of AI programs are progressing quickly, but they're not so close to human imagination that you couldn't tell the difference. At least, this one isn't."

"Let's give it one more test," said Danny, leaning over the bench and reaching for the keyboard. "The issue is imagination, isn't it? Think of how Mary Shelley used that word, and of the Paris students' mini revolts of 1968."

"Is there anything you don't know?" said Rick, chuckling, but now determined to find something that Son of Hubert could say to get the better of Danny. He gave Danny a friendly shove and took back control of the keyboard. So how inventive could Son of Hubert be, he wondered? He typed a command:

I want you to write a story about artificial intelligence, with the title: 'Unleash Your Imagination'.

GRC, March 2023

The Director Smiled

THE DIRECTOR SMILED. IT WAS THE FIRST TIME HE HAD
done so today, and it was an inscrutable kind of smile, lacking
humour or warmth. He motioned to Suzanne to sit down in front
of his polished mahogany desk. He liked to keep the whole office
a little dark, with concealed lighting on the heavy bookcases

behind him and a low overhead lamp playing on the desk and the seats in front. That way, he could see his visitors' every move; every twitch, without revealing much about himself.

Suzanne was the Assistant Director of Human Capacity Development at BBM, an Australian mining conglomerate based in Collins Street, Melbourne. As she was fond of saying, in the old days she would have been called the Personnel Manager, but these days 'personnel' was too impersonal. We're all human beings, after all, whatever our gender, colour, religion, sexual orientation or able-bodied-ness, and whatever our competence, paranoia or intolerance level.

Suzanne looked the Director in the eyes. He was a well-proportioned man in his late sixties, neatly suited, and with an air of authority that few would dare cross. He was responsible for finance and a number of other areas of the company, including personnel. As she waited for the precise questioning she knew was coming, she noticed his face relax from the unfamiliar smile. Worn lines re-formed into that lived-in face he had worn for the past twenty years in top-level management. His eyes drilled into hers, unblinking.

"Your note said you have a problem with Kaliotis?"

"Right you are. I have to confess, I've seen a few oddballs in my time," she began, "but Nick Kaliotis has me whacked. If he'd gone troppo or something I could take it in my stride, but the bloke's attitude is mystifying."

"Tell me more." The Director had an air of patience, as a panther does when stalking a deer.

"Nick's a typical Greek Aussie. Hard-working, keen to get ahead, very tight with family, and as loyal and honest as you could reasonably expect a corporate lawyer to be. Serious-minded – no larrikin. But he point-blank refuses to comply with the company's Covid vaccination policy."

"What did he say exactly?" asked the Director, his lined face graver than ever.

Suzanne looked at her notebook. "I wrote it all down exactly as he said it. His exact words were 'I'm not having some American crap bunged in me arm. No way, José. They don't know what's in it, you know. Cut corners everywhere to get it approved. You can't trust the Yanks.' That's what he said. Word for word."

"Strong stuff," the Director responded. "You did explain to him, I guess, that if we can't get the vaccination levels up to scratch, the company could fail? It means we can't reopen half the offices, or of course the mines and the labs. Disastrous." He was looking for Suzanne's ideas; something to bring about a swift resolution. This was not the only fish he had to fry today: a finance meeting was due to take place in five minutes' time.

"Sure thing. I was very clear on that. I also pointed out that his view was getting round the bush telegraph, influencing others. Very disruptive. I wondered if there was some cunning way to bring him round, but he was adamant. And when a lawyer has a fixed view on something, you can bet there's a lot of thought behind it – it's hard to change their minds."

"Your call, Suzanne. I have plenty of other things to concentrate on this week. See what your team can come up with. And meanwhile, I suggest you have a direct and challenging talk with him – maybe outside the office."

Suzanne did not relish the task, but knew it had to be done. She turned to leave the room, took a deep breath, and nodded at Julia, the finance head, as they passed in the doorway. Julia did not look happy either.

*

Suzanne sat on a stool in the gallery of a new coffee shop on Elizabeth Street. Her team had spied it out and told her that this was a regular spot for Nick Kaliotis to buy lunch. With the lockdowns over for the time being, the cafes could allow a small number of dine-in customers, although most were still buying food to take away. She laid her sunnies on the bench in front of her, alongside her cappuccino. Her position at the edge of the gallery offered a great view past a potted plant down over the main part of the shop, where the heads of half a dozen socially distanced people bobbed about in the process of ordering and collecting drinks and salad rolls. Everyone behind and in front of the counter wore masks. Outside, the crowds were thinning, sauntering past, trying to keep cool. A tram went by, clanging.

As Suzanne had hoped, she saw Nick come in through the main door to the downstairs service area. He didn't stand out in a crowd, but she noticed the neatly folded handkerchief in the top pocket of his immaculate suit, which matched his tie. While he was standing in line to order his coffee and sandwich, stroking his thick head of neatly trimmed grey hair, she kept staring at him. This would be the opportunity to talk informally – she needed to get this right. As he paid, he glanced up, and she smiled, beckoning him to join her. He climbed the stairs slowly, reluctantly, and sat down on the stool next to hers, still holding his coffee as he put his sandwich on the bench between them.

"G'day, Nick," she began in a friendly tone, not wanting to appear threatening. "Look, mate, I wanted to talk to you."

"Okey-dokey, let's talk, then."

She decided to cut to the chase. "You know everyone's very happy with the work you do," she began, looking directly into his eyes and smiling. "You're a very effective operator. You've been a shield for the firm, even in the courts, so I hope you don't mind me bringing this up again."

He shifted uncomfortably but made no move to leave or to help her out.

"I really don't understand where you're coming from with all this stuff about the vaccines, and in my role just now, it's frankly bloody difficult. I need to know that our senior people understand what really matters to the firm. The Director is mad as a cut snake with you."

Nick didn't seem surprised; just looked down at his coffee with a half-smile. "There's too much going on," he said, shifting again on the stool and putting his coffee down at last. "It's more than what's happening at BBM, it's more than this country. It's the whole world, you know? They're after us. They're after the whole world. They want to take it for themselves."

Suzanne thought this sounded completely insane. The guy was obviously paranoid, but on the other hand he was a very competent lawyer and had got the company out of a number of scrapes. He had made sure that infringements of their patents did not go unpunished. He made settlements with plaintiffs that would otherwise have caused great embarrassment to the company and risked its reputation as well as its finances. He was no fool and no bludger. He was educated to postgraduate level, so why did he have these extraordinary beliefs? "You need to explain this to me," she said firmly, leaning forward and narrowing her eyes. "Are you telling me that your views on vaccines are driven by something bigger: your fear that some mysterious forces are trying to take over the world? Doesn't that strike you as being more than a little...strange?"

"Bigger, yes. It's not so simple. Look, I'll be more open here, 'cause there are no ears flapping like in the office." He looked around, bobbed his head, and looked up at her briefly. "Maybe you'll get it?" He sucked in a breath. "It's not as simple as that, but yes, I suppose the fact is that you can't trust anyone. You certainly can't trust governments. The pollies and all the parties are in on the conspiracy. Defo, you can't trust the international agencies: the WHO, the UN, the World Bank, the IMF – they're all in on it, y'know."

"'It?' What do you mean?" she responded indignantly, rocking back on her stool, her voice losing some of its cool. "Come on – surely as a lawyer you can see that you can't just blurt out such bald accusations as facts without any evidence? The international agencies are run by people from all over the world: different creeds, nationalities, ethnicities, political opinions – whatever. You can't seriously suppose that they all have some common purpose to do damage to mankind, and particularly to you?"

"Well, I hope you're right. I hope there is no one out there doing these things, but I know you can't trust them. You can't trust any of them. They have their own agendas. They're working on things we know nothing about. Look at people like Gates and his vaccine programmes, and some of the others. Look at Musk. They're all doing things we don't know about: some of 'em going up there in space, spending so much money. Where does it come from? It comes from us, the consumers. Every cent they get comes from customers buying something."

"Well, I wouldn't argue with that." She could see the limits to people making money at other people's expense. "I'm not too happy about the billionaires and their antics myself, and I reckon they should be feeding some of their money back into good causes – positive feedback – like Gates does. But that doesn't mean they're out to get rid of the rest of us. It makes no sense, does it? Then there would be no consumers to fund them, would there?"

He continued, ignoring her logic, and facing her with his right hand spread out on the bench. He hadn't touched his sandwich. "There's some other agenda that he's following with his fellow billionaire mates. They all get together at Davos, you know. They talk about these things."

"Come on, Nick! There's no evidence at all that they're plotting a world takeover – the discussions at Davos are widely publicised. Now, let's get back to the vaccination programme – that's what matters for BBM."

"They're gonna give this country back to the Abos, you know. Talking about giving them a voice in Parliament. They've been doing it for thirty years: apologising, giving back land, granting all sorts of privileges. The rest of us, the Europeans – we'll just get pushed into the sea."

Suzanne went quiet. This was another unexpected turn, and a very dangerous one in the current political climate. That kind of view from a senior person at a major Australian company…no way. She remembered the distaste when the Prime Minister at the time, John Howard, had abolished a commission charged with protecting Aboriginal interests. Now there was a move to include the rights of indigenous people in the constitution to provide some reliable protection – and about time too. That was hardly people of European heritage being pushed into the sea.

"You have to agree," Nick went on vehemently, leaning forwards, and Suzanne pushed back her stool to put some distance between them. "We don't know what's in the vaccines. People are dying all over the place from the side effects – ethnic European people, mainly. They rushed it through. There can't have been proper trials."

Suzanne was getting rattled. Another set of wild assertions based on no evidence. She shook her head and let out a long sigh. As it happened, she had an old university friend attached to the Oxford group developing the AstraZeneca vaccine, so she knew how hard they had been working, and how they had managed to cut through the financial red tape that often held up the development of vaccine batches for initial trials. That was why it had progressed so quickly; it was not due to cutting scientific corners. "Now, there I know you're wrong," she countered, staring him straight in the face and wagging a finger at him, her voice rising. "I've been through all this. I had to check that it was safe for our management to recommend vaccinations, and I checked what the Health Department was saying in the scientific literature. I even spoke with people I know who are close to the developments. I've checked the actual numbers. People are *not* 'dying all over the place'."

"Well, I don't know much about science or numbers. I only know what I hear from those who are doing their own research."

"Huh! I would suggest that's a big part of the problem." Suzanne's arms dropped to her sides as she shook her head vigorously. She had heard that phrase before. 'Doing their own research' could just be a euphemism for spreading malicious gossip without evidence. How was a lawyer being taken in by this anti-scientific posturing? He of all people should understand what constituted evidence. She was trying not to lose her cool. "Look, Nick, all of the scientific data goes against what you're saying. If you look at reliable journals like *Nature* or *The BMJ* or *The Lancet* you don't find any of this stuff, but you *do* find refutations of it. All the data goes the other way: the vaccines are already saving millions of lives worldwide. So where are you getting your information from?"

"You know I got a brother in the States, don't you? It's all in my file, I'm sure. Some of my info comes from him. He's connected with the right groups: the groups that are fighting this. He was supporting Trump, but I don't know whether Trump's part of the conspiracy. Maybe he is? But some of the people who supported the anti-vax movement, they know what's going on and they're trying to stop the worst of these things happening."

"But there's no sign of any of the things that you're predicting. There's a few cases of bad reactions to vaccines – a minute proportion. That's unfortunate, but normal with any medicine. There's no sign of massive reactions causing a reduction in the world's population. Despite all the wars and epidemics, the population is still rising. Do you realise, by the way, that this whole scenario of a virus cutting the population is the theme of a Dan Brown novel from a few years back? I think that's probably where they're getting it from. There's no sign of any of this when you look at reliable data. You're insulting brave, efficient and hard-working scientists because of some bosh off the internet from people who are about as sharp as a bowling ball."

"Well, I hope you're right." His tone was respectful, but he obviously didn't believe that he could be wrong.

To Suzanne he seemed like a member of a religious cult: stuck with a belief system that was impossible to prove and very hard to disprove. At this rate, it was going to cost him his job, and then he would paint himself as a martyr: the dark powers would have got him. She shook her head and breathed out sharply. She was truly exasperated, and felt that she had to leave before she started shouting at him. The guy seemed to be delusional as well as an out-and-out racist, and neither was acceptable. Australia had more than its fair share of racists, but she was not going to collude with such views. If that came out, the press would have a field day and BBM's share price would suffer. The board would go apeshit. She gulped down the remnants of her coffee and waited a few seconds before standing up and grabbing her sunnies. "Sorry, Nick, I have to get back. We're going to have to go through this a bit more, because what you're saying in the office is disturbing a lot of people. You know as well as I do that you're very valuable to the company, but you're driving a herd of brumbies through company policy. That, to be quite frank with you, is a career-limiting move. You're making things difficult for everyone. People are talking about it. There have been written complaints."

"Well, let them talk. Someone's got to stand up for us ordinary people. We've been here for generations now and they're trying to push us out. We gotta do something about it."

*

Back in her office, Suzanne was boiling with frustration. Here was an intelligent, highly educated bloke; maybe lacking in numeracy and appreciation of science, but he should know about evidence. He should be looking at the facts from reliable sources. Instead, his distrust of authority was making him think about evidence in terms of the plausibility of the witness – it was medieval. And for some unknown reason, he had persuaded himself that the ramblings of some American right-wingers who were friends of his brother were more reliable than the WHO. It was preposterous. He didn't even have a weird personality. There'd been nothing odd in his Myers–Briggs profile. He was polite, efficient, not pushy; unusually smart for an Aussie bloke, perhaps. Thankfully, he wasn't talking to anyone else about the racial angle. No one had mentioned that; just that he was refusing the vaccines, rubbishing their effectiveness, casting doubt on their safety, and telling people he didn't trust the manufacturers or the agencies that had approved their use.

Much to her distaste, she would have to follow up on this. If he refused to show some solidarity with senior management, well... And she would have to administer the blow. He was becoming a danger to his colleagues and to the company, so she would have to read more carefully through his personnel file for any indications of trouble, and start collecting detailed evidence for a dismissal before giving him a formal warning.

She remembered some advice the Director had given her when she'd taken her job. "Think like a chess player – what's the next move if you fire someone?" When the subject was a high-profile lawyer with a great track record, how much damage could he do? Plenty.

It was worth another try to get him into line...if she could keep her emotions under control. Now that the restaurants had reopened, albeit with distancing rules and limits on the number of diners, perhaps an evening discussion over dinner would provide the right kind of atmosphere to get him to see sense.

*

A few days later, Suzanne and Nick were sitting together in the upstairs restaurant at Bluetrain on Southbank near to the casino; Melbourne's desperate 1990s recovery scheme which had turned out to be quite successful.

Nick joked about it. "Ha. Chockers in here! Or at least as chockers as it can get while we're social distancing." He peeled off his mask. "Southbank is quite a place," he began cheerfully, his hands locked together in front of him on the table. "A monument to Jeff Kennett's gambling-and-prostitution-led recovery!"

Kennett had been the Premier of Victoria when the Southbank renewal project was conceived. Miles of crumbling warehouses had been transformed into trendy bars, restaurants, upmarket apartments, and a casino over a kilometre long. Both Nick and Suzanne had seen the development blossom when they were teenagers, and Suzanne remembered the dares she and her friends had had with each other to run through the pavement water jets which intermittently fired spouts up into the air, resulting in an instant drenching if you were in the wrong spot. The kids still loved to do that.

"Yeah. It's quite a place," she echoed, remembering the part it had played in her courtship with her husband, Ken. She would have dearly loved to be at home curled up with him, rather than spending an evening trying to persuade this weird bloke to see sense. The discussion began. "Look, Nick, I suggested meeting here because you said you prefer to talk out of the office."

"Right! This is sensitive stuff, and who knows who's listening there?"

She didn't respond – another provocative remark. Did he really think the offices were being bugged by Bill Gates, Elon Musk, the Director, or some covert CIA activity?

"I mentioned the Abos when we had that chat at the coffee place. It's all part of the same thing. There's a plot. Been going on for thousands of years. The billionaires, the governments – they're out to enslave the lot of us and get rid of European types on the way. The vaccine is one way they're going to manipulate us. They've put something in it."

Suzanne was already starting to get riled, but her mood was lightened a bit by the distraction of the waiter arriving with the menus. Wanting to get on with the discussion, she could feel her heart pumping after Nick's first salvo. They ordered quickly. She was thinking of her Oxford friend working all night in the clean room at the lab to produce minute quantities of starter vaccine, and then having to go straight into a TV interview in the morning. There was no way anyone was influencing them. They were doing it because they wanted to save lives. And they were succeeding. As the waiter moved away, she glanced around and noticed one of Ken's colleagues a few tables away, in animated conversation with a girlfriend.

Suzanne was struggling to remain calm, but looked Nick directly in the face as she spoke. "What evidence have you got that 'something' has been put in the vaccines? That's a well-known and thoroughly debunked conspiracy theory."

"There's no such thing as a conspiracy theory," he responded, leaning back in his chair with an air of confidence. "That's something made up by the CIA in the '70s to control the masses. They make it sound like someone is organising all these 'conspiracies', but the opposite is true. The apparatus and the machine exist on the other side – the conspiracy theory thing is pure bullshit. It's basically trying to kill the critical thinking of regular people."

"Oh, come on, Nick. Conspiratorial thinking is a well-known phenomenon. We all want to make sense of what goes on in the world. These people whose posts you read on social media are trying to lock you into their ideas and make you scared – and they make money out of the clicks. There's no way that all the reliable sources – scientists, government, international agencies – are conspiring against all the ordinary blokes out there. Your brother's friends are trying to make sense of social and natural forces – like the pandemic – that are hurting them, and they feel threatened. That's why they see false connections between events and famous people or racial groups. It's just human psychology. I don't understand why someone like you – a good lawyer – doesn't see through this stuff."

Nick shook his head. "These people know who's being shut up. They know the vaccines don't work. They're killing people."

"What people? Where?" she responded, raising her voice.

As the conversation started to heat up, two waiters appeared with their food – a Caesar salad for her; steak and chips for him – and the mood relaxed a little.

"Great tucker here," he said, smiling at her and cutting into his steak. "They're hiding the truth," he continued quite calmly, spooning some pepper sauce onto the meat. "You won't see it in the media. The 'fact-checkers' censor it all. They're just young journos straight out of school. Don't know what they're doing."

"Look, Nick, I've checked the fact-checkers. I go back to the original sources, and they're usually right." She stopped dissecting her salad in its bowl and looked up at him.

He backed off, avoiding eye contact and glancing around the room. "Well, I just hope you're right. Next year is going to be the showdown. Armageddon."

"Do you know how many times Armageddon has been forecast? How many times in the last fifty years? Fanatics have made those predictions many times before, and they've always been wrong." She was speaking a touch above normal pitch, and one of the waiters sidled past, obviously listening, but absently pressing buttons on his mobile.

"More and more are prophesying as it gets closer. My brother gives me the links. I trust him."

Suzanne put down her knife and fork and breathed out slowly while looking Nick in the face. Anything that she said in the way of facts that could be proven by science or by investigation, he would deny. For each fact there seemed to be an alternative fact that was more acceptable to him. How a lawyer could think this way was beyond her. This kind of evidence would not stand up for ten seconds in a court of law. "And who are these mysterious people that are feeding you misinformation via your trusted brother? Do you know any of them?"

"Nope, maybe not. But they sound bonzer to me: smart websites, TV interviews. It all adds up. All the little things. The country people understand because they're not brainwashed like us townies."

Shaking her head, she started eating again, musing on the situation and holding back any instant response. A lot of this problem was the fault of social media. It sounded as if Nick was following extreme sites that his brother put him on to. Redneck material, by the sound of it. But in a country like the US with 330 million people, there were bound to be plenty of extreme views. It was just bizarre that this bloke whose life had been built on the certainties of Melbourne and its suburban culture, and who had never even associated with rural poverty, could come up with such a strange set of beliefs. Especially when it seemed that he could function perfectly normally in his working environment, apart from the vaccination matter. He was religious, too – but the Greek Orthodox Church didn't espouse those views. Suzanne had read only recently that all the churches in Australia were supporting justice for the indigenous people.

She noticed Ken's colleague catch her eye. He was smiling, and she smiled back, trying to look calm. Maybe she was speaking too loudly. At least there seemed to be somebody sane in the room. But then you think about it – seventy million people voted for Trump. They can't all be nutcases or white supremacists. And lots of other populists have taken power in recent years. People get pushed into supporting pollies who seem to be offering them some comfort, regardless of whether that comfort will be delivered. Is it just individual charisma that causes ordinary people to get caught up in belief systems that are quite insane? There was a lot going through her head.

"Are you following someone in particular?" she asked. "Some leader who peddles these disproven ideas? You don't seem to think much of Trump, so is there some other leader you're following?"

Nick avoided the question, but picked up on the word 'disproven'. "Oh, you're listening to the fact-checkers – young kids just out of school. They don't know what they're talking about."

"Young kids just out of school with PhDs in data science and psychology and access to original peer-reviewed research, you mean?" She was almost shouting. That was too loud. The conversation at nearby tables stopped for a few seconds. She forced herself to calm down.

"I know what I know." He stared glumly at his plate and spiked a piece of meat with his fork. "I have a clear feeling about this. I'm quite sure something bad is gonna happen, and it's all down to these vaccines. They've got hold of the process and they will make sure that the vaccines get administered to everyone in the world. Then in five years' time, everyone is gonna start dying." He looked up with a serious expression and leaned forward as if vouchsafing a critical clue. "It goes back to that professor from Harvard who sent the virus to Wuhan, where the institute was conveniently built in 2009 by a French founder of Moderna. It's a picture with too many pieces. People are putting all this together, connecting the dots, because it's out in the open, and the fact-checker kids can only suppress so much. Then what most people miss and don't understand is the *why*. It's a lesson: stay as alert as possible and away from this government advice. Do your own homework."

"Look, those so-called 'kids outta school' are not easy to fool because they're very bright and have access to most of the primary sources. And that's what they're looking at, you know. They're nearly always right, if you bother to look."

He responded with a stock answer. "The media don't let us see what's really happening. The media are part of the scheme. They're trying to lead us away from the truth so we can't see the rug being pulled out from underneath us."

"Why do you think that? What evidence do you have? If you were in a court of law and you were trying to prove that case, what proven facts would you bring up? Nothing you've said gives me any impression that you have real material information behind this. You just have rumour, innuendo, half-truths and circumstantial occurrences that you're weaving into some huge plot. This really doesn't make sense. Why can't you see it?"

"It's bigger than us, babe," he said smugly. "These people have been planning it for generations. They've just got you fooled. You haven't got the real facts about these vaccines."

She stood up, prepared to make an exhibition of herself, and did so loudly. "Are you calling me a liar?"

The whole restaurant was silent by now. One of the waiters standing by the door focused his attention on them and turned, ready to march over quickly in case something worse was about to happen.

Nick's phone went off. He muttered, "Must take this," and strode onto the balcony, past Ken's mate and the alerted waiter.

Suzanne sat down, feeling foolish, and fiddled with the food in her bowl. She had let her anger with his condescension, his deluded viewpoint and his disrespect for science get the better of her. The atmosphere calmed as the diners resumed their conversations, like waves demolishing a sandcastle. She concentrated on making some notes on her phone about her own conversation with Nick.

He returned after about five minutes, his face flushed. As she looked up, she noticed that Ken's mate and his girlfriend had gone.

"Sorry, Suzanne," Nick started contritely. He sat down and adjusted his tie, putting his phone down gently on the table. "I was winding you up a bit." He took a sip of water. "Look, I know I've been causing some trouble, and I can see it's putting you and the management up shit creek. I've made a decision. I'll shut up about the vaccine thing, at least in the office and with company people."

Suzanne stared at him, her face softening, realising that she had won the battle, if not the war. He was going to comply – a sudden change of tune, but she guessed he now believed that she had the power and the guts to fire him. Maybe her angry outburst had achieved something after all. At the end of a negotiation, she remembered from a training course she gave regularly, when you have got what you wanted, it's best to shut up and leave before anyone says anything that might change things. "Oh…right… Well, that's good. That's really good, Nick. That's gonna make a lot of people very relieved. Sorry I shouted," she concluded sheepishly. But she was wondering who had called him, and whether the call had anything to do with his decision now. "I think we should pay up and go. Halves?"

"Sure."

Suzanne signalled to the waiter, and he brought the card machine over.

"Was the food OK?" said the waiter as the payments went through, noticing that neither of them had finished their meals.

"Yes, fine," they chorused, and smiled at each other briefly before walking out of the door and turning in separate directions.

*

When Suzanne got home, Ken was uncharacteristically sitting at the table, reading something on his iPad and sipping tea. It seemed a little odd. By this time in the evening, he would normally have been in front of the TV, watching sport of some kind. As she came in, he stood up and looked at her with a quizzical expression.

"I was talking to Jeremy a few minutes ago, my colleague from the university – you know him. He said that you were at Bluetrain tonight with a guy from the office. He said it sounded like you were having a bit of a barney."

"I told you I had to talk to a colleague about a personnel matter."

"Well, seems like it was quite heated. I mean, that's not like you at all – must be a big issue. Is there anything I can do?"

Suzanne was taken aback. She and Ken lived reasonably separate lives, professionally speaking, and there was never any question about who could have lunch or dinner with whom in a work context. But this seemed to be different.

Ken spoke cautiously. "Jeremy said you and some smart-looking guy seemed to be engaged in a very intense convo. I know I can't ask what it was about because he's an employee of your company and you're in charge of personnel, so I guess it must be some matter of that kind. But doing that in the evening at full volume in a busy restaurant? Perhaps that's not a great idea."

Suzanne's first inclination was to become defensive, but then she realised that the meeting had been quite a success in the end, and she should be pleased with herself. She had acted foolishly by getting wound up, though, and she could understand Ken's concern. It *was* unprofessional. But her objective had been to try to resolve the strange conundrum of Nick's delusions. And it seemed she had – rather unexpectedly. "Oh, I know, darling. It was a tough situation." He looked puzzled, so she continued, "You know, it's a personnel thing. But maybe I can talk in the abstract and you can put your psychologist's hat on to help me with this?"

He started to look a little more comfortable.

"Just maybe, it has worked out… OK, I lost my rag and that was stupid. But then he had to go out to take a phone call, we both calmed down, and he kind of changed his tune."

"OK, darling, just tell me what the circumstances were without naming the people involved and I'll see whether there's anything I can suggest. When you're really close to a situation it's hard to see what's going on."

"OK, my love – fancy a glass of red?" She poured two glasses of Penfolds Shiraz, put them on the table and sat down opposite him. "It's a tricky problem because it's about people's beliefs. There's one bloke – a senior bloke – who's against the vaccine campaign. I needed to understand why, because if we can't get the company back to full strength the shareholders are gonna start losing money and we're gonna be in the shit."

"Ahhh, caught up in the vaccine conspiracy theory?"

"Well, yes." She stopped to gather her wandering thoughts. "That made me mad because I know the efforts my Oxford friend and the group in that lab have made to get the vaccines out there double quick. He's disrespecting all that work."

"Yes. That pisses me off too. A lot of people all over the world have dedicated themselves to that work for months. Now I'm starting to see why you got so angry."

"But it's more than that. There's a racist element. He's against indigenous rights and thinks some mysterious forces are trying to push the whites out of Oz. These days, most Aussies can see that dealing with the wrongs that were done to indigenous people is an important thing for this country. Or at least, most of the ones I know can see that. It's important that communities come together, and that kind of talk is not gonna help at all. If a senior employee of our company starts spouting off like that it's really gonna do us a lot of harm. Thankfully, he hasn't been saying those things in the office."

Ken nodded as if this phenomenon was not new. "Yes, that's not unusual. I understand something of the psychology of this. It's known as apophenia."

"I thought the psychology community would have a word for it."

They both chuckled, and Suzanne took another swig of red.

"Some people perceive meaningful connections between unrelated things, and build up elaborate castles in the air. Some end up living in them. They're often the dupes of some really nasty people who use fear of the unknown to leverage the gullible into supporting some very dubious causes."

"That's our bloke all right – influenced by crazies on the internet."

"It's very hard to get people out of these beliefs, especially these days, when social media fosters and shapes our ideas: people share their delusions, and the positive feedback they get strengthens those delusions. It's like a religion. They can't see the inconsistencies. They constantly shift the goalposts when you hit them with a rational argument. But eventually a lot of them do come to see sense."

"Maybe that's what happened tonight?"

"Well, I wouldn't be too confident about that. This is hardcore stuff – he may be playing a game. A lot of these anti-authority things come with a white supremacy angle. It's known as the Great Replacement conspiracy theory. I guess he doesn't trust authority much. Is he religious too?"

"Yes; distrusts authority and he's religious. He seems to think Armageddon is on its way and the pandemic is part of it." She sipped her wine. "Mmm. The Coonawarra reds, always good…"

"Ripper," he said, swilling the red liquid around his big glass. "And is he a gut-feeling merchant: not focused on logic or numbers?"

"Well, yes. In fact, he's got the company out of a couple of scrapes because he's good at connecting the dots."

"Is he a social media guy? Maybe thinks his group doesn't get enough consideration? Quite a good dresser – looks the corporate part?"

"Yes. Exactly. You sound like you know the guy."

"Not exactly." Ken put down his glass and looked at her. "But he ticks all the boxes."

Suzanne was intrigued. "And…?"

"There seem to be some common characteristics of people who get caught up in these theories," he explained. "It's true of some religious people and political types too. They believe they can see things others can't see. Often can't grasp the difference between correlation and causation. When events happen in sequence, they believe there's intention behind them – someone causing the events – so they make a chain of cause and effect. It's usually fantasy, but not always. That's why these types can often rise high in organisations and politics. They're intuitive managers, rather than scientific or analytical ones. Sometimes not very numerate."

"So they see things like the pandemic and the fantastic scientific response to it as part of a big plot?"

"Exactly, but they can never offer any convincing evidence. Their way of thinking is just to point at arbitrary anecdotes that support their view and ignore those that don't. Then they try to rubbish the other side's arguments. Like lawyers in a courtroom."

Suzanne looked up sharply, fearing that she had said too much. She tried to make her discussion more abstract. "Yes, I know that the anti-vaccine theories tie in with the anti-authority thing, especially in the States, but this is the first time I've seen it all close up. They really think someone is organising all of the world's events for a purpose."

"Exactly. Got it in one. Often the theorists are not experienced at managing people and don't know how difficult it is to get any bunch of individuals moving in a similar direction, even for a few months. Sometimes they identify the conspiracy with some famous person – often Bill Gates in this case. But of course, nothing is being decided by anyone from the top down. What happens in the world is the combination of all the decisions eight billion of us make every day. The planet is a complex, adaptive system, and it will evolve by trial and error."

"Mainly the latter," added Suzanne.

"Right. Resisting change according to Lenz's law – you know, complex systems react to minimise the effect of an external change. So the global situation is the usual complete shambles because individual politicians have too much power and try to make changes without thinking through the psychology of them. Meanwhile, there are internet grandstanders who are making money from advertisers as their number of clicks goes up. It's in their interests to make things look as scary as possible. In my view, they have nothing to add and are part of the problem, not part of the solution. The scientific community – not just Gates – have been warning about the risk of massive pandemics for many, many years."

"Wasn't there a Hollywood film or several, a few years back – *Contagion*? I remember being scared of the fruit bats in the Botanic Gardens for months after that."

"Right! In reality – and this is the big point – people are not the protagonists, nature is. Lenz's law – it's as if the planet is trying to reduce human impact. Not consciously, of course, but at the base level of physics and chemistry. Imbalances get corrected. It doesn't need a plot. Nature just does its thing according to natural processes. Sorry for the lecture."

"Yes, I understand the logic. It's similar to the superstitions people have about spirits in trees and sacred mountains – lots of anecdotes, but they ignore the misses and only look at the hits. Like my grandmother's terror of pins."

"Pins? I'm intrigued," said Ken, taking another sip of the Shiraz.

"It goes back to medieval superstitions, I suspect, when they had these crazy fears about sorcery. They were burning witches in Europe until the late eighteenth century at least, if I remember rightly. People believe the strangest things and get caught up in mob fantasy. Without a good understanding of science and numbers the world must have seemed very frightening. I guess we should have some sympathy for them." She was quiet for a minute. "So at the end of his call, this bloke just comes back and calmly says he was winding me up and he'll stop being anti-vaccine at the office. I guess he twigged that I was prepared to fire him if he didn't support the firm's policy. The Director had already given me the authority to do it."

"Well, that might scare him, but these are usually people who will cut off their nose to spite their face. It would make him a martyr if you fired him."

"That's what I reckoned." She swirled the wine in her glass, suddenly feeling quite conspiratorial in the warm mesh of a supportive relationship. As her fears retreated, the familiar, comfortable feeling of trust re-established itself. "I'm not fully convinced he'll do what he said, though. It was very strange that he backed off so suddenly. I've had at least three meetings with him where he was adamant. Perhaps I'm getting too distrustful?"

Ken was sympathetic. "I agree, it does seem odd. I wonder what might be behind it? I would watch him carefully. If he fails to live up to what he said he'd do, I'd take it straight to the Director and get the bloke out of there."

"Well, let's hope he sticks to what he promised this evening. Then my part of it will be at an end, I hope." Suzanne looked distant for a moment. "I tell you what, why don't we put together a few of the figures on the vaccines in case he backtracks, or in case there are others he's convinced already? I can get a slot with the senior management to take them through it all and ward off any rearguard action. I'm still a bit suspicious, though: there could be something I'm not seeing. Anyway, thank God it's Friday tomorrow." She yawned.

"Come on, gel. We'll do a bit of research of our own over the weekend." Ken stood up and put out his hand.

She took it and let him pull her up from the chair into a long kiss.

*

Suzanne was waiting outside the door of the Director's office as he finished a meeting on production targets. She and Ken had worked on a few slides over the weekend that demonstrated clearly that vaccinated people had less than twenty per cent of the chance of catching the disease compared to unvaccinated people; and something like a ten per cent chance or less of dying from the virus if they actually got it. The scientific evidence on the vaccine's effectiveness was incontrovertible. The safety figures were just as good, despite some adverse outcomes which were mercifully very rare.

She was called in after a few minutes. In the office she explained the situation and showed the Director some of the figures. Nick did not have a leg to stand on regarding his opposition to vaccination. She didn't go into any of the embarrassing details about what had happened at their last meeting. At the end of it, he had capitulated, she said, and agreed to stop championing his views in his dealings with other people at work.

The Director smiled. "Bonzer result, Suzanne. So we should be able to get the vaccination figures up to scratch. That's a big relief. We can open all the factories and offices again, and although there's some hard yards to come, we should be on course for a profitable year. Well done."

"Thanks. Just doing my job," she said humbly, but inside she was buoyed up. "I'll put the vaccination data on the advice website so the staff can see it."

"Yes, and maybe you could do a presentation to the executives early next week, so they all understand the basics?" He glanced at his on-screen diary. "Why don't you do it next Tuesday? There's a senior management meeting in the morning then anyway. We could bring it up as an agenda item. Then I could give you about half an hour? That will get everyone on the same page."

"No probs." She smiled and stood up. She had got exactly what she'd wanted from the meeting, and she turned towards the door.

"Oh, just one thing," the Director added, raising his eyebrows a little. "Do you think Nick's tied in with some group here in Melbourne? One that's pushing these anti-vax ideas or other conspiracy theories?"

"No, he says he's getting a lot of it from his brother in the States. The brother does seem to be connected with a few galahs who are defo away with the fairies, but I don't see anything in the discussions I've had with Nick that suggests he's meeting with any fellow weirdos here in Melbourne. I would have heard if any of the racist stuff was going round the office. People complain about that."

"Racist stuff?" The Director raised his head sharply, looking concerned.

"Yes, he's getting stuff from his brother on white supremacy and such – he told me that."

"OK. But there's no racist conspiracy angle here in the office, right?" said the Director, standing up to indicate that the meeting was over, and clearly not wishing to get into a discussion on such sensitive matters. "Just check out if there's any remaining disruption among the staff, particularly in the clerical areas. Those are the places where we need people to be fully vaccinated. You'll have to get your team doing a few calls. We've still only got a skeleton crew on the ground, as you well know."

*

After the senior management meeting, Suzanne felt confident that the vaccine conspiracy problem had been laid to rest. She got home early for once and made some pasta. When Ken arrived home from the university, they sat down to eat their meal and she ran through the events of the meeting.

"I explained how conspiracy theorists see a pattern in the misinformation being fed to them, but they can't chart the steps and show how the connections work. And I went through the data we put together about vaccine safety and how it's clear that the vaccines have saved millions of lives. The executives responded well and there was some positive discussion."

"That's good," Ken remarked, looking pleased about Suzanne's success.

"Then I drew the conclusion that we've lived through a massive human disaster that has been mitigated by quick and effective scientific work. And a host of doomsayers are disrespecting what's been achieved, often to make money for themselves. That's the real conspiracy."

"I'm proud of you," said Ken, tucking into the pasta.

They settled down to a quiet evening binge-watching a Netflix series, stretched out together on the sofa.

*

After the management meeting, the Director had walked to his car and driven a few blocks towards Richmond. There was a Greek restaurant there that he liked. Nick was sitting towards the back when he arrived.

"Well done, mate. I know that was tough for you," the Director began, pulling out a chair and sitting down opposite Nick.

"Yeah. You can say that again. That sheila's quite something. I thought she was going to ram a fork down me bloody throat. Good job you called at that moment."

"No coincidence, mate. I've got me eyes."

"Ah, well, I owe you one," said Nick quietly. "I'm really scared, you know. I don't know when people will start dying. My brother's friends keep telling me it's going to happen soon. I don't have anyone to talk to, you see, except for my bro, so I just go over and over it. I'm not good with numbers, I just know – down here…" He patted his stomach. "I can't let them get away with it. In court it's easy. The crooks back off when they know you got them sussed. But this – they're everywhere. I just tried to do something. I'm sorry."

"On the contrary, I know it's hard for you to back off from your public view on the vaccines. And you have got people thinking, as we expected – a few have talked to me privately and I've explained the real issues, so they'll be with us on that. That's been a useful outcome of your concerns. But the vaccination thing was going a bit too far from our sponsors' point of view, so I had to set Suzanne on you to keep it clean or I would look weak. You don't have to do it, though: I can fix the paperwork. Everyone else can decide for themselves. Look, it's going to be OK. We've got enough influence with the powers that be to keep ourselves safe, even if the playing field is tipped against us."

"Yeah. I guess I was mouthing off too much."

"Right, mate. That was a close call – you'd better be less vocal. We'll look after you, but don't play with fire. I know it worries you a lot, but the vaccination problem is a bit of a distraction from the real thing. To be honest, I'm not convinced about these long-term dangers. I'm a bit too much of an old geezer to worry about that kind of long term in any case. So right now, I've got to get the vaccination numbers up – at least on paper – to make sure BBM can get back into profit this year. Otherwise, we're all down the dunny. But that's as maybe. You know what we're really fighting for – and that's today."

"Yeah, I get it, boss. We gotta keep our country pure. Stop the indigenous rights crap in its tracks."

"Right, mate." The Director stood up, clapped Nick twice on the shoulder, and walked straight to the door without looking back at his foot soldier.

Nick waved anyway.

As he pushed open the door, the Director smiled. Everything was back on track.

GRC, August 2022

The Abyss of Possibility

DENNIS MILLER WAS A LIKEABLE BUT RATHER ORDINARY man. Until the age of sixty or so, he had lived a pretty nondescript life: underestimated and underemployed, with a few close friends and the memory of his fading youth. His one marriage – to a lady who regarded him as grey and boring but herself as glamorous and deserving of social advancement – had ended painfully and expensively. All he had left from that time were frequent bills and an Om tattoo on his neck that she had insisted he have during one of her New Age phases. He enjoyed his books and his jazz albums, and he loved his garden, but the English weather was not kind to his collection of tropical orchids that he kept in his small greenhouse in the warmer months and indoors in the winter.

Then suddenly – or so it seemed to his friends – he decided to forsake his South London council house to live in the cheaper environment and pleasanter weather of Thailand, where his small pension would stretch further. It was a big move for him, but he was confident because he already had the entrée to a circle of friends and a cool music venue.

About three months before, he had received a birthday call from an old friend, Vince, who had set up a new life in the Land of Smiles a few years back. Vince had been one of Dennis's closest friends, and their shared passion for music had been a source of pleasure for both of them. During the call, Vince had talked enthusiastically about the place. He said he had fallen on his feet in Thailand, found a gorgeous wife who told him he was "handsome man", and fulfilled a life's ambition by opening a jazz cafe in the market area of a pleasant coastal town: the Jazz Bar in the Casbah. He urged Dennis to join him, hoping that they could renew their meeting of minds on the finer points of Miles Davis and John Coltrane; at least for a few months so that Dennis could work out whether the place suited him for the long term. With such an offer, Dennis thought more and more about leaving the miserable cold and damp of England for more attractive pastures, until, having few ties to his native land, he took the plunge.

Maybe I'm a sharper bloke than people think? he thought, laughing to himself as he sat in a window seat on an A380, squeezed next to a big, sweaty man and gazing down at the turquoise crystal of the Andaman Sea.

*

Before long, Vince had introduced Dennis to his wide group of friends. Dennis had become a regular at the Jazz Bar in the Casbah and had rented a small house with a little garden so that he could be surrounded by the tropical plants he loved.

On his first New Year's Eve in the country, he found himself on a beach with Vince and many revellers, setting off large oblong-shaped lanterns with a wick inside them, which enabled them to fly into the dark sky with the aid of hot air. The scene was unspeakably beautiful. Hundreds of lanterns flying out over the sea on a gentle breeze. Friends around, and an awful lot of Chang beer inside. Before crossing the road to the beach, he had enjoyed a pleasant New Year's Eve dinner with his friends, most of whom had their Thai wives with them, but Dennis was alone. Since separating from his social-climbing wife years before, he had never been one to mix himself up in romantic engagements. In Thailand he was happy to gently play the field and enjoy the company of whoever was willing to be with him for a short time without binding commitments. Now, after launching his lantern and noticing that it was already 1am by his watch, he decided to bid farewell to Vince and the crew and set off for home.

"Mind the pit vipers," yelled Vince cheerily. "And I don't mean your ex!"

A chorus of "Cheers, mate" and "*Sa bai dee pi-mai*"[1] rang out in a range of European and local accents.

Dennis walked unsteadily along the beach for a while, and then took a turning that led towards his house. It was quite dark, and he knew that he was considerably the worse for wear. As he

---

1   'Happy New Year.'

was stumbling along, looking carefully at the ground to avoid any pit vipers, he heard a vehicle behind him approaching at speed. When he turned to look, its lights blinded him, and he just had time to leap out of the road as a pickup truck rushed past, its tyres showering him with gravel. He grabbed at a tree trunk to avoid falling into the ditch beyond and continued to clutch the trunk for a few moments afterwards, recovering his breath and shaking his head in annoyance.

Then, looking down, he noticed something glinting in the wan pool of light shed by a nearby street lamp. He leaned unsteadily into the brush at the bottom of the tree to pick it up, and instantly dropped to his knees. Worrying about the pit vipers, he seized the bole of the tree again to right himself, then he could see the strange object better. It looked like some kind of brass lamp. His thinking was somewhat confused by his alcohol-soaked evening and after his near miss with the truck, but nevertheless he bent down and grasped the object. He was opposite one of the town's market areas, now silent and dark, not far from the Jazz Bar, and he guessed that this object had fallen from a stall, or from one of the many trucks that had supplied the previous day's market. It seemed like a trinket sold from some handicrafts stall, so he picked it up and carried it with him. It was elegant: a traditional oil lamp shape, but with intricate designs on the brasswork. It would look rather nice on his shelf with the souvenirs he had picked up during his few months in Thailand.

When he reached his door, he spent some minutes fumbling with the key; then finally as he opened the door he tripped and sprawled over the threshold. The lamp flew from his grasp. He couldn't be bothered to look for it, but pulled himself up, drank some water to recover a bit, and slumped into a chair. There he slept fitfully for a while, and at about four o'clock in the morning, when it was still very dark, he realised where he was and took himself off to bed to sleep properly.

*

It was about midday on New Year's Day when he woke up. His head was befuddled from the previous night's excesses, and for a while he did not remember the lamp. When he did recall it, he searched for it, and eventually found it under the settee. As anyone would in those circumstances, he gave it a quick rub with a duster to get the grime off and to see how the brass would shine up.

This is where the story gets a little more difficult. There are thousands of genie stories and genie jokes – yes, you rub the lamp and out comes the genie and offers you your three wishes. Dennis was not expecting anything like that. But nevertheless, that is exactly what happened. Musky white smoke issued from the spout of the lamp as he rubbed it. The lamp became hotter, and eventually he had to drop it among a lot of rubbish on the coffee table – newspapers, coffee cups, banana skins, pizza boxes and so forth. The lamp was the latest addition to the debris. Nevertheless, the smoke continued to pour forth, and from it a humanlike creature formed, shimmering in the vapour and solidifying until it stood on the table among the detritus of the past few days.

The creature was about five feet tall – and obviously a he. Quite small for a genie, thought Dennis, so taken aback that he didn't feel taken aback at all. But then he thought again. Wait a minute – this is not possible. There can't be such a short genie, and certainly not a genie standing on my coffee table. What on earth is all this about? Am I rather more under the influence than I thought I was? Is this just some kind of hallucination? I remember reading about things like this in books by Oliver Sacks.

Drugs and drink can make you imagine entire conversations with friends that never actually happened.

He was roused from his reverie by an incoherent, squeaky voice, which clearly emanated from the genie. By this time, the genie was a well-formed apparition – a stereotypical Disney genie with all the genial accoutrements: an Arabic-looking face; a turban; medieval Middle Eastern clothing; and turned-up slippers in the Turkish style. This was certainly a full-blown genie visitation. Dennis was, to put it mildly, gobsmacked. How could this have happened in the twenty-first century, when we're living in the age of digital streaming and Pot Noodles? His mind was churning. The idea of an unexpected apparition popping up and granting wishes was something he had never considered to be remotely plausible.

Suddenly, the genie's voice seemed to pull itself together and to make sense. He had been gabbling in an incomprehensible tongue, but now he moved into remarkably modern London English. "OK," he said. "OK, I get it, squire. I know where I am. I know who you are and I know where you come from, so I'll speak English to you – *comprende?*"

Dennis's mouth hung open. A faint gurgle came from his throat.

"Now, listen," said the genie. "I haven't got all day and you know the deal. It's three wishes, right? No more, no less. Three wishes, that's what you got, so let's get on with it, shall we?"

Dennis pulled himself together a little. He was still unsure whether this was real, a dream, or a hallucination. His heart was beating unusually fast. "Well," he said lamely, "you'll have to help me here. I've never been in the presence of a genie before and I'm not quite sure what I should do, what I should say. Perhaps you could give me a little guidance?"

"OK," said the genie, tapping the toe of one of his emerald-green slippers a little impatiently on the coffee table. "Yeah, I know it's difficult. Yeah, we know the problem, us genie types. You appear to somebody, they ain't got no idea what's going on, they think they gone nuts. But no – N-O. This is all pretty standard stuff. Here we are." He tried to shake a bit of Wednesday night's pizza crust from one elegant shoe. "I'm a genie," without pausing, he scraped the congealed pizza topping off his shoe onto the edge of Dennis's table, "and I'm here to grant you three wishes, all right?"

"Well, that's great," said Dennis cautiously, warming to the occasion but still overcome by incredulity. "I mean, really that's…that's great. I could do with three wishes right now. I could wish…" He stopped suddenly, realising that as soon as he said 'I wish blah-blah-blah', the genie would grant it, and then he might regret what he had asked for. Instead, he turned his gaze downwards as if trying to find inspiration in the cheap nylon rug. "Just give me a chance to think, will you? This is all a bit of a surprise – a shock, in fact. So let me think about it. Let me – no, *don't* let me come out with something stupid that I'll regret for the rest of my life."

"Yeah, yeah, I understand," said the genie, "but we haven't got all day, you know. Let's get this show on the road." The toe-tapping started again. "But OK, I'll give you a couple of minutes to think about it and then come back. Now, I want three clear wishes, right? Wish one to wish three. So you sort that out, have a think about it, and I'll deal with it. Oh, and by the way, have you got a bathroom here?" He hopped, or kind of floated, down from the table.

"Wait a minute," said Dennis, even more flummoxed. "You're a genie, aren't you? An apparition from the spirit world? What do you need a bathroom for?"

"Oh, come on. You can see I'm in human form, can't you? Or I'm a kind of human being, anyway, so I have natural functions, right? So be so good as to tell me where the bathroom is. I'll just be away for a few minutes, so you can have a think and then I'll come back and we can sort out these wishes, all right?"

Dennis was bemused. "The bathroom's just over there. So pop in, use whatever you like, and I'll be ready for you when you come back."

"OK," said the genie, hopping from foot to foot. "Off I go, and no looking through the keyhole, right?"

"I wouldn't dream of it," said Dennis, amused by the cockney banter.

Suddenly feeling extremely sober and rather sharp, he was getting excited about his three wishes. He might as well play along with whatever was going on. He had to think it through. Wow, what could they be? What am I really concerned about? This really makes you get your life into focus. There were problems in my past, like the ex-wife who is still always bothering me for money so she can impress her friends. Problems in the present, like this small, untidy house. I could do with somewhere smart, somewhere really nice…and maybe a housekeeper to look after me. Then one of those Mercedes SUVs would be nice. Maybe something like that? And… Wait a minute, I've got an idea. It may be that this genie is not quite as clever as he looks. Maybe I could get better value from this deal? A bit more bang for buck, as it were, through a particular kind of wish? Maybe I'll try it. Dennis had heard a lot of genie stories and remembered one in which the victim – if that was what he was – had tried to outsmart the genie by making his third wish 'To have three more wishes'. But the genie had put him into a time loop, so he kept having the same wishes over and over again. No, that would never do. Dennis had to be careful how he worded his third wish. He made some notes on the back of an envelope he found lying on the table under a mouldering apple core.

The genie came back into the room, coughing a bit and doing up his flies. He had changed out of his medieval Arabic outfit and now looked like a rock star, with long blond hair, no turban, and a bit of a swagger. He also seemed to have grown about a foot and a half, and was now well over six foot. Around the waist of a pair of stylish distressed jeans, he wore a cowboy belt. Dennis thought he smelt tobacco smoke.

"Have you been smoking in there?"

"Why? Why do you wanna know?" said the genie, looking a little sheepish.

"Well, I don't allow smoking in my house."

"Look, you got a genie here in your gaff offering you three wishes. For once it's not someone trying to stitch you up. Life changin' stuff, innit? Are you really gonna worry about being politically correct at a time like this?"

"No, no," said Dennis, rowing back quickly on the PC bit. "I really want these wishes and I've got an idea of what I want now, so can we sit down and talk about it?"

"Right you are," said the genie, sitting down in a threadbare armchair with some semblance of good humour. "I don't usually sit down on the job. I usually waft round the room, and actually, I often stand on the table as it makes me look taller. Sometimes I just materialise in wispy smoke and stay there, but I reckoned in this particular case, with this being quite a nice place and a bit hot anyway, I thought to myself, why don't I materialise more fully and stand on the ground, as you see me now? I also wanted to try out this new outfit, because I thought you might be the kind of bloke who'd appreciate a more modern style. Do you think it's good?" He stood up and sashayed around a bit before sitting back down and crossing his legs stylishly.

"Well," said Dennis, trying to be complimentary to his potential benefactor despite the extraordinary circumstances, "you look a bit like Roger, the guy who plays guitar down at Vince's jazz bar from time to time. But I have to say, you do seem a bit more handsome. Even a little dashing, maybe? And quite a bit younger... I particularly like the cowboy boots."

"Oh, well, thanks very much. I appreciate that. It's not often you get compliments in this job, you know, so it's good to hear someone say something nice to me for a change. They're usually so bloody grasping... But nevertheless, I don't wanna hang around. There's every chance somebody else will be needing me in a few minutes, so let's get on with it, shall we? What's your first wish?"

"OK," said Dennis, slowing the tempo and looking carefully at the piece of paper in his hand. The genie's warning about someone else making a wish in a few minutes' time had gone straight over his head. Cautiously, he tapped the envelope with a pencil; then he looked the genie in the eye and spoke firmly. "This is my first wish, and I've written it down so I can get it absolutely right. Maybe you already know what I'm going to ask, being a genie, but I imagine you know my circumstances already."

"Ah, yeah, yeah. I know most of what's going on in your life. It's a mess, really, innit?"

"Yes, it is, really," said Dennis, crestfallen that the genie could write him off quite so thoroughly. "I've made a few mistakes in my time, but perhaps the biggest one was my ex-wife. She's really been a big problem for a long time. Always asking for money, and I can't afford the maintenance. She's one of the reasons I came out here. It's cheaper to live, so I can afford to pay what she's asking for. Now, if you, Mr Genie, can make that requirement for payment go away, I think that would really help me."

"Look, don't call me Jeannie. I've got a name, you know."

"Oh, really? That's interesting," said Dennis, raising his eyebrows in surprise. "So what's your name, then?"

"It's Mike."

"*Mike?*" said Dennis incredulously, wondering since when genies had been called Mike.

"Just stop whingeing, will you?" The genie had clearly had some embarrassment with his name before. "I mean, I can choose what name I like. I'm a bloody genie, aren't I? Don't you go moaning about it or thinking it's funny. It's my name, innit? Now, come on, let's get on with this. Right, you want your former wife to stop asking you for money, is that it?"

"Yeah, that's exactly it," said Dennis. "I want her to stop bothering me for money."

"Right. Sorted. It's done – she won't bother you any more."

"What? That was quick," said Dennis suspiciously. "You haven't had her killed or something, have you? That's not what I wanted. I just wanted her to stop bothering me for money. In a funny way, if she died I would miss her."

"Look," said Mike the genie, looking Dennis in the eye with a businesslike expression. "You asked for a wish. I've granted it. Stop complaining, will you? It's not easy doing this stuff, you know. I mean, every day I've got someone asking me for some amazing bloody wish, and I have to go and do it, don't I? It's part of the job description, so I can't avoid it. But it's up to me what method I choose to grant the wishes, so stop complaining."

"But I didn't want you to kill her."

"Now, come on," said Mike, clapping his hand to his brow. "It's not your business what method I use to stop her asking you for money. You might find something slightly surprising about what actually happened, but nevertheless, she won't be asking you for money any more. So is that all right with you?" He raised a quizzical eyebrow. "Now, your first wish is granted – come on, give me a bit of feedback, a bit of positive affirmation and all that."

"Thank you," said Dennis, looking down at his envelope with the wishes scrawled on it with a suitable degree of humility.

"That's better," said Mike, stretching out his legs and leaning back in the chair.

Dennis was completely floored. This conversation was not quite what he would have expected from a genie. There was an awful lot of answering back, and not so much of the 'Your wish is my command' stuff as he'd been expecting. What had the guy been smoking in the bathroom? Nevertheless, if he would no longer be bothered for money (and hopefully not just due to a straightforward matter of extinction), then perhaps he was getting somewhere.

"OK," said Mike, gently but firmly. "What's your second wish? Get on with it."

"Well," said Dennis, preparing his words to counter a bit of pushback, "my second wish is a bit more like your average wish from a genie – you know, a wish for something good. I want something nice for myself, something to make my life more comfortable and to give me a bit of financial freedom to make sure I'm not going to be unhappy here."

"Yes, yes, I see." Mike sat forward in the armchair and looked a bit exasperated at Dennis's slow delivery. "Come on, then, let's get on with it. So you were grumbling about financial freedom and stuff, but what do you bloody want?"

"Sorry. OK. What I want is this. I want a much finer house than this, with all the services. Everything working properly, no leaks in the roof, and a housekeeper to look after it. Oh, and I'd also like a new Mercedes GLA in the yard, if that's OK by you."

"Oh, hang on there, hang on there just one moment, squire." Mike was looking half amused and half irritated. "That isn't one wish: that's three wishes, innit? You wanna house, you wanna housekeeper *and* you wanna posh car. That's three wishes, not one. So do you want just one of those wishes, or do you want to combine two of them into the two wishes you've got left? What do you want to do?" He stood up and wagged an admonishing finger at Dennis, who tried to remain poker-faced. "Huh. You can't fool me, you know." The genie seemed entertained by Dennis's valiant attempt to up the value of their arrangement a tad. "You're trying to get more out of this than is available under the deal. I thought better of you than that. Do you think I was born yesterday? Actually, it was my 5,349th birthday last Wednesday, so you can cut the wise guy stuff."

Dennis could see that Mike was not a genie over whose eyes he could easily pull the wool, as it were. He had to be a bit more careful with the way he phrased his wishes. So what was it that he wanted? Did he want the nice house? Did he want the nice housekeeper more than the house? Or did he want the really smart car that would make his friends very jealous? There could be a problem with houses and cars, and perhaps especially with housekeepers. There's a lot of legal business around these things, particularly in a country where the bureaucracy is a little hard to follow because it's all conducted in a language that's not entirely familiar. "OK, Mike, you got me there," he conceded. "I'll go for the house. Just give me a nice house in the same place, a bit more land, and everything in working order."

"Well, you know you're still stretching it a bit, to be honest, but I'll give you that, all right? I'm getting to like you, so I'll be generous."

Dennis was a bit flattered by this, but some sixth sense warned him that Mike's affection was as feigned as that of a barrow boy in the market back in South London. Although maybe, in challenging him a bit, he was giving the genie a chance to enjoy the game a bit more than he usually did.

"I'll give you a bit more land and the great house, and make sure the house won't have anything wrong with it," Mike continued. "I can give you my guarantee as a genie – and that's a three-year warranty you've got there, so you're not going to have problems with this house for three years. Now, just close your eyes a minute, will you?"

Dennis noticed a strange roaring sound, but he kept his eyes closed as instructed. When he opened them, he found he was in palatial surroundings. The house was beautiful: cool, modern and stylish. There was fabulous polished teak woodwork everywhere, subtle grey tiling on the floors instead of the old lino, subdued lighting, and a kitchen with all the appliances he could wish for. Everything was tidy; no more newspapers and pizza boxes all over the place. Everything absolutely pristine. There was a wonderful stone-topped table with dining chairs. A huge sixty-five-inch TV screen with all the latest smart-TV gadgets on it. The view outside the window had improved as well. The scrubby area beyond the previous wall had vanished and turned into a beautiful garden with large trees and colourful birds flitting between a host of exotic flowering plants. "Wow," he said, standing up and looking around, his arms akimbo. "This is fabulous. This is exactly what

I wanted. Thank you so much, Mike – this is brilliant. I'm very happy: so far, things have gone really well."

"Yeah, well, of course. I'm a bloody genie, aren't I?" Mike had a bit of a smile on his face as he ran his fingers through his rock star hair. "That's what I'm here for: to make you happy. To give you your three wishes. So you've had two of them, all right? And although you haven't seen the results of the first one yet, you can be sure that it's going to be to your advantage. You just said you like the beautiful house, so that's good. I'm very happy for you. That's great, so let's get on with it, shall we? What's your third wish?"

Now, this was where Dennis had had his brainwave while the genie was in the bathroom. He was going to ask for something that would tie Mike's powers to him in a way that might be somewhat unusual. "So," he said expectantly, "this is my third wish. I wish that you would reappear whenever I want you to, granting me three wishes again and again and again. But they have to be different wishes, whatever I want – no cunning stuff like time tricks or anything."

Mike was silenced. It was clear he was a bit confused: he stood up, and his appearance seemed to be alternating between the five-foot-high Arabic-looking genie with Middle Eastern gear and the six-foot-five rock star. The two were blurring and merging with each other. After a few seconds, rock star Mike reasserted himself and prowled around the room for a couple of minutes, muttering. He poured a glass of water from the new water-filter machine and leaned on the kitchen counter, gazing in Dennis's direction and sipping gently. Dennis stared at him anxiously. Maybe he had tried to be too clever.

"Well," said Mike at last. "This is a bit unexpected. To be honest with you, I didn't think you were that bright, Dennis.

You see, what you've done, matey, is what we in the trade call 'the hat trick'. You've asked for something to do with the past, something to do with the present, and now you're asking me to do something about the future. That's a bit of a problem from the quantum electrodynamic point of view, you realise. According to my job description, I've got to grant you three wishes, so that's two wishes you're happy with. The third one? Yeah, very clever, Dennis, very clever wording. Nicely laid out. I admire you for that brilliant stuff, especially as you sorted it out while I was in the bathroom for five minutes.

"But now matey, this gives us a bit of an existential problem, doesn't it, because you're asking me to change the future. Changin' the past and the present, that's fine because they're there already, so I can go back and sort them out. But changin' the future? Well, you never know what's going on in the future, do you? So it's not so sure quite what's gonna happen. You might be asking for more than you think, because if I just turn up whenever you want me, then anything might be happening. You know, I could be in the middle of a poker game somewhere and you suddenly say, through some sort of transformational quantum funnel in space-time, 'Mike, come here and sort out this small problem for me', and there I am, you know: I've got four aces and I'm pulled away from the bloody table and I'm gonna lose a fortune. Or I can think of even worse situations for a genie, you know, but I won't go into that."

Dennis felt that he was starting to get the upper hand in this conversation, especially since Mike had gone back to metamorphosing every few seconds between the rock star and the ageing Arab. It looked as if there was a short circuit going on somewhere in the genie dimension. Nevertheless, Mike pulled himself together and got his feet literally back on the ground, rather than floating about a foot above it in his Arab guise, which was where he had been a few seconds before.

"So are you going to grant me this wish?" said Dennis more confidently, leaning back in his chair and clasping his hands together. "So I can bring you back any time I want to fix whatever problems I have with another three wishes? 'Cause that's my wish."

"Then you're asking for a kind of recursive genie experience, is that right? You want to have a wish within a wish, within a wish, any time you want to wish a wish within a wish, as it were?"

"Yeah, you got it. That's precisely what I want." Dennis sat forward and looked Mike in the eye, although the genie was towering above him. "I want to be able to call on you in the future whenever I need you, so that whatever problem I have, you can grant me three wishes and I can find a way through it."

"Mmm," said Mike thoughtfully, strolling back to the water filter and refilling his glass. He leaned on the counter again, sipping enthusiastically. "I think you fail to see the problem with that proposition in terms of the stability of time. What I mean is," he waved his now empty glass vaguely in Dennis's direction, "I reckon there's a way that I could grant you that wish. Although I might well have to go back to headquarters and check it out with the powers that be and so forth. Specifically, those who run the time business. But nevertheless, I can think of a way that we might be able to do it. However, it will need you and me to do a deal. A different kind of deal. Oh, yes!" He grinned, which seemed a little sinister to Dennis; then he put his glass down carefully on a coaster, showing some care for the new furnishings, and strolled back to the armchair.

"OK." Dennis was guarded, watching the genie's moves and grasping the reality that it was 1 January and instead of formulating ridiculous resolutions – ones he would immediately break – he was contemplating doing a deal with a spiritual apparition that would no doubt be a lot more demanding. "What kind of a deal are you talking about? Do you mean you need me to do something for you every time you do something for me?"

"Got it in one, Dennis. You really are brighter than I thought – especially considering what you did last night – but yeah, that's about it. I'll come back to last night, by the way. There's a couple of things I know, but you're not aware of," said Mike mysteriously, cocking his head to one side and widening his eyes. "You have to realise that, if you want a lot of wishes from me, then you've got to do a few things for me as well. And sometimes they might not be quite the sort of things you want to do. You see, somebody else might ask for a wish and I might have to get you to do something in order for that wish to come true. And that might not always be pleasant, you know?"

Dennis didn't have much time to work out the implications of this proposition. A deal is a deal. And a deal done with a genie who knew the past and the present – and probably the future too, if he had a chat with the time guys – was almost certainly going to be hard to get out of. Dennis knew a few lawyers, but he didn't know any who dealt with contractual relationships with beings from the shadowy worlds, even if those beings wore cowboy boots. There could be all sorts of issues concerning intellectual property, professional indemnity and so forth; issues he had no idea about. As far as he was aware, the lawyers he knew didn't know anything about those things in the pan-chronologistic dimensions, as it were, either. It had certainly never been a topic of conversation over a few beers down the pub. "So if we do this deal, Mike, how is it going to work?" he asked. "How will I know when you need me to do something?"

Mike chuckled. "Oh, you'll know all right, Dennis. There is no doubt at all that you will know when I ask you to do something. You will be very clear what it is you have to do, and if you don't do it then that's the deal broken and you'll never get my help again. You might find that somebody else has asked me to do something that might not be in your best interests, shall we say. You could find yourself staring into the abyss of possibility."

Dennis didn't like the sound of that, but Mike was still explaining.

"You see, the abyss of possibility is that sinking feeling you get when you have the freedom to choose what you're gonna do. Isn't it easier, matey, to live with your decisions being set by somebody else's requirements and never have to make too many choices for yourself? That's what I'm implying."

Dennis was beginning to realise that he could end up in a position where he was controlled by the genie's other clients, and all because he had forced Mike into a position in which his existence was circumscribed by Dennis's third wish.

"Think of it this way," said Mike, sitting forward in the armchair and gesturing towards Dennis, who was paying rapt attention, "if I grant you your wish, then you are in my power, although by granting your wish I'm putting myself in your power as well. Is that the kind of relationship you would like to have with a spirit from an unknown world? You know, you only met me this morning and now you're about to commit your life to any requirements I have, in the same way as I will be committing my existence to any whim you have about calling me back to grant you more wishes. We will be like two entangled electrons at different ends of the universe, whose spins are coupled so that when one moves, the other must move too."

Dennis was not fully familiar with the theory of electron entanglement, but thought it best to let it go.

"If I grant your wish, it's almost as if we become one being. You will be the genie, because you can call up my help at any time to get what you want. But I will also be you, because I can influence your free will to get you to do whatever I need you to do to meet the needs of other people who've asked for my help."

This was not the kind of conversation that Dennis had been expecting to have on the morning of New Year's Day, or at least the afternoon. He'd thought that he had cleverly devised a wish that would bring the genie into his power whenever he needed support. But there was always a quid pro quo, and the implications of that were completely unknown. Completely unknowable. Dennis's mind was running so fast, he could hardly keep up with it. What could possibly go wrong? Just about anything. But as a man already in his sixties, he was unlikely to get the offer of such a deal ever again. Would it help him to live a longer life? A happier life? A more fulfilled life? Or would it mean that he would be just as much at Mike's beck and call as Mike would be at his? "Look, Mike," he said, scratching his head and looking squarely into the genie's dark eyes. "This is a very profound decision you're asking me to make. 'The abyss of possibility' seems a fine description of the dilemma you're putting me in. It's not a step, it's a dive into the darkness."

"Come on, matey. *Me* putting *you* in a dilemma?" said Mike. He stood up, strolled across the room, and resumed his leaning position by the water filter, looking back at Dennis with a degree of irritation. "Look, it's your wish. If you wanna change your wish and have the Mercedes, then do so. But if I grant you the wish – the wish that you've asked for – then there will be repercussions and responsibilities that'll go with it and you won't be able to get away from them."

Dennis shifted uncomfortably as Mike stopped lounging on the worktop and strolled towards him, his knowing grin back in place, looking, Dennis thought, as if he were holding all the cards.

"But don't let me scare you too much. It won't all be downside," continued the genie, folding his arms and smiling serenely. "There will be plenty of good moments: travel the world, meet new people for deep and meaningful experiences – that kind of stuff. Live for 5,000 years."

Dennis drew in a sharp breath.

"Like that moment last night, when you missed treading on a pit viper by about five centimetres. It was when you leapt out of the road 'cause that pickup was speeding by. You could have been bleeding to death and in terrible pain before you even found that old lamp. Nothing's certain in this world, is it? Not even in mine it isn't. The abyss of possibility can open up at any moment." Mike chuckled, smiling at Dennis in a way that intimated both riches and risk, like a spymaster exhorting his agent. "So you've already crossed a bit of a threshold, old son. Think about that – and decide."

Dennis nodded. He suddenly felt light-headed, and could see himself, as if from above, sitting on the sofa with Mike towering above him. His vision was extraordinarily clear: edges sharp; colours bright. Time seemed to pass slowly. A dog barked loudly nearby.

"Oh, I wish that dog would shut up. I feel so peaceful here."

It did. It was just beginning to dawn on Dennis what Mike had meant about tangled electrons being a single system when there was a knock on the door. Almost instantly, Dennis was back on the sofa feeling fine, and Mike was nowhere to be seen.

*

None of the guys had heard from Dennis all day. Remembering the state he'd been in at the New Year's Eve celebrations, Vince wanted to check that everything was OK, despite his own quite stressful day. It was just getting dark – about six o'clock or so in the evening – when he came round to see Dennis. He knocked on the door. There was no answer, so he knocked again. There were some noises inside the house, and Vince noticed that there was something different about the outside of the building. It looked a lot bigger, and in much better condition than he recalled. It was then that he noticed that the scruffy little yard with tired orchids everywhere had expanded into a huge and rather beautiful garden. That was rather strange. He was wondering if he was in the right place when the door opened. There was Dennis, looking sprightly.

"How are you?" said Vince, advancing into the house as Dennis beckoned him in. "The guys were a bit worried about you after last night. You left the beach party looking a bit shaky. After you said cheerio and wandered off, we didn't know what happened to you."

"Well, it's OK. I'm fine. In fact, I'm really very fine. You know, I feel more energetic than I have in ages. I think this is going to be a good year. Why don't you take a seat, Vince, and we'll have a drink, and we can talk about what's going to happen next?"

Vince came into the living area and was astonished by the change from what he remembered from his last visit, which had only taken place about a month before. The whole open-plan area was tidy. There were new kitchen units and machines – good-

220

quality ones. There was a huge new TV screen, a wonderful table, and comfy sofas. The place looked immaculate. Absolutely beautiful. "Have you got a new housekeeper?" asked Vince.

"No, no, no," said Dennis. "I've just been doing a bit of tidying up and I got a few alterations done recently which you might not have seen before."

"Well, they look like pretty dramatic alterations if you ask me. You must have spent a fortune on this. How did you do it?"

"I have my methods," said Dennis, glancing sideways with a secretive smile.

"And I like those cowboy boots you're wearing," said Vince as he sat down on a rather beautiful leather sofa that he was sure he hadn't seen before. "Dennis," he began, sounding as if he had something important to say, "I don't know whether you heard, but something strange has happened to…you know…that ex-wife of yours."

"Oh yes, really?" Dennis widened his eyes, sounding as if he had been expecting this turn in the conversation. "So what's happened to her?" To Vince he looked only mildly surprised that there was some news about his ex.

"You mean you haven't seen the papers or the TV?"

"No," said Dennis, trying to look more surprised. "What do you mean?"

"Well, knowing what she used to be like years ago, back in London, I don't know how she could have done it, but she's only gone and married one of the richest men in the world. Look…" Vince whipped out his phone and showed Dennis a news article.

Dennis sat back and laughed long and hard. "Yes, I heard she's been with a guy for a while. Someone – a friend, you might say – told me about his new inventions for space travel and such. Very well off, they say! Well, good luck to her. Let me make you a coffee." He sauntered over to the kitchen, rubbing the Om tattoo on his neck and leaving Vince looking at him strangely. "Anything else going on after the New Year revels?" he asked as he brought the coffee over.

"Yes, I'm afraid there was something else," began Vince. "There was a bit of a fuss down at the market this morning. Some guy was tearing the place apart looking for some brass ornament he'd lost. The police had to come and take him away. He was calling down curses on all and sundry, something about 'falling into the abyss of possibility'."

"Oh, sounds nasty. Was it near the jazz bar?"

"Yes, unfortunately it was. He broke the big window and wrecked the woodwork. I'll have to shut up shop and get it fixed. Thought I'd get the place redecorated too and make a couple of changes while I'm at it. It'll mean having to close for a few days. Not a good time of year for that – high season an' all."

Dennis glanced at the shelf by the side of the giant TV and saw the lamp glistening there. He hoped Vince hadn't noticed it. He changed the subject, hoping that he might be able to do something to ease his friend's stressful day. "I'm going to take a holiday, Vince," he said, waving an arm dismissively towards the exquisite furnishings as if he was sure that he could find something even better. "Thailand is lovely and I'm very settled here, but I fancy three weeks on one of those Mediterranean beaches with pure white sand and crystal-clear turquoise water, a small boat bobbing in the bay surrounded by verdant cliffs, islands in the distance, a beautiful young woman lying next to me on a comfortable lounger, and a wonderful beach bar with great food and any drink you can think of."

Vince's eyebrows shot up in pleasure thinking about this evocative scene. "Very poetic, Dennis. Oh, what with all that's going on here, that's just what I'd like too – I wish I could have a holiday like that."

*

Vince woke up because it felt as if his legs were being ironed. He grunted and sat up. The sun had shifted during the morning and was now beating down fiercely on his thighs. A small traditional fishing boat bobbed gently on the clear water in front of him. Its name in Greek was θαυμα – *Miracle*.

Lazily, the young woman lying next to him opened an eye. "How you doing, Vince?" she crooned in a kind of mid-European accent. "I'm getting hungry."

Instantly he knew that her name was Isla, and the whole history of their happy five years together. There was something worrying him slightly, but he couldn't put his finger on it for the moment, so he pushed it aside. "Let's go over to the beach bar," he said, waves of contentment flowing over him.

"Sure thing, honey." She got up and wrapped a towel around her glorious body.

They could hear the soft tones of Greek rebetika music emerging from a pair of large speakers as they turned away from the sea. Hand in hand, they sauntered the few dozen yards to the bar, where a barman in dark designer shades was sitting in front of the counter, casually polishing glasses. He beamed at them and stood up, glass in hand. He was over six foot tall, very muscular, and seemed happy to see them. Vince noticed that he was wearing cowboy boots and, unusually for a Greek, his long hair was quite blond. Vince vaguely thought he recognised him from somewhere, but maybe that was the niggling worry. There was a sixty-five-inch screen showing Euro football on the back wall, and an incongruous but inviting leather sofa under an awning. Lying on the sofa was a book entitled *Readings in the Homeostatic Balance of Time: Part 1.*

"*Kalispera*,"[2] said the barman. It was, after all, past twelve o'clock. "I am here to serve you. Your wish is my command." He had the warm, fluid accent of a Cretan. He stopped polishing the glass for a moment, smiled broadly, and rubbed an unusual tattoo on his neck. Then he took off his shades and looked directly at them with startling dark eyes.

"I am Michaelis," he said, "but you can call me Mike."

GRC, November 2022

---

2   'Good afternoon.'

Acknowledgments

I would like again to thank my literary friends Richard Skinner and Gary Rutland, who have continued to encourage me on my literary journey and have read a number of these new stories and given me valuable editorial advice. Thanks also to Richard for organising a mini marketing tour of the English West Country where we had a great time showcasing my first volume of short stories *Someone Else's Gods*, Richard's novel *Still Crazy...* and his short story collection *After All...*. We are hoping to do another series of events in the UK when this volume and Richard's *These Years: 1973* are published in 2024.

I would also like to thank my literary editor Lesley Hart who has again been able to help me to improve the quality of the stories significantly while making sure I avoid non-sequiturs, inaccuracies, anachronisms and lawsuits.

I am grateful to Jeanette Bourke, Phaedra Clarke and Maritsa Clarke for guidance and advice on specific stories, where their points of view were important to ensure authenticity; and to my Aussie mate Rob Groves for advice on the correct usage of *Strine* slang. And also to many others who have inspired stories by their dogged perseverance through adversity or their determination to hang on to outlandish beliefs in the face of all the evidence.

Helen Hart and the team at SilverWood Books have continued to provide great support in the logistics of publication, adding value in copy-editing and proofreading to ensure all quotations and foreign language terms are correct and that familiar phrases, quotes and terms have been used within the Society of Author's Guidance on Copyright and Permissions. The publication journey has been somewhat easier the second time and that is largely due to the organisational skills of the SilverWood team.

My everlasting thanks to my partner, Tue, who has looked after me not only through the painful process of completing a manuscript for publication and meeting deadlines for other professional demands, but also through the challenges to health and wellbeing that afflict those who have lived long and eventful lives.

Finally to those who have bought and enjoyed *Someone Else's Gods*, I am most grateful for the kind and constructive comments that I have received both from friends and more anonymously through Amazon and Goodreads. The positive feedback has undoubtedly helped inspire me to complete *The Abyss of Possibility*.

You can see more of my work on www.manandcyberman.com.